"You've decided to ask for joint custody, haven't you?" Cara whispered

"I think I've come up with a better solution," Ross told her. "It's a little unconventional, but…"

"You can't take my children away from me. I won't let you."

"No. I'm not staking a claim on your children, but ideally the children should be allowed to grow up together."

"I thought you said you wouldn't try to take them away."

"What I'm suggesting is more of a…merger." He hesitated.

"A merger?" Cara's brow furrowed.

"Of families. Yours and mine."

She blinked. "I don't understand."

"I think we should get married."

Dear Reader,

Welcome to another month of wonderful books from Harlequin American Romance. We've rounded up the best stories by your favorite authors for you to enjoy.

Bestselling author Judy Christenberry brings readers a new generation of her popular Randall family as she returns to her BRIDES FOR BROTHERS series. Sweet Elizabeth is about to marry another man, and rodeo star Toby Randall will let nothing stand in the way of him stopping her wedding. Don't miss *Randall Pride*.

An injured firefighter and the woman he rescued in an earthquake learn about the healing power of love in Charlotte Maclay's latest novel, *Bold and Brave-Hearted*. This is the first book of her exciting new miniseries MEN OF STATION SIX. In *Twins Times Two!* by Lisa Bingham, a single mom agrees to a marriage in name only to a handsome single dad in order to keep together their two sets of twins, who were separated at birth. And enemies are forced to become Mr. and Mrs. in *Court-Appointed Marriage* by Dianne Castell, part of Harlequin American Romance's theme promotion THE WAY WE MET...AND MARRIED.

Enjoy this month's offerings, and make sure to return each and every month to Harlequin American Romance!

Wishing you happy reading,

Melissa Jeglinski
Associate Senior Editor
Harlequin American Romance

TWINS TIMES TWO!
Lisa Bingham

HARLEQUIN®

TORONTO • NEW YORK • LONDON
AMSTERDAM • PARIS • SYDNEY • HAMBURG
STOCKHOLM • ATHENS • TOKYO • MILAN • MADRID
PRAGUE • WARSAW • BUDAPEST • AUCKLAND

To all parents of "multiples." Especially Will and Erin.
Congratulations on the adoption of the triplets!
How your family has grown!

ISBN 0-373-16887-X

TWINS TIMES TWO!

Copyright © 2001 by Lisa Bingham Rampton.

Visit us at www.eHarlequin.com

Printed in U.S.A.

ABOUT THE AUTHOR

Lisa Bingham is a resident of Tremonton, Utah—a rural farming community where the sounds of birds and the rustle of wheat can still be heard on hot summer evenings. She has written both historical and contemporary romances and loves spending time watching her characters grow. When she isn't writing, she spends time with her husband on his three-hundred-acre farm and teaches English at a local middle school.

Books by Lisa Bingham

HARLEQUIN AMERICAN ROMANCE
602—NANNY JAKE
635—THE BUTLER & THE BACHELORETTE
651—THE DADDY HUNT
662—DANA AND THE CALENDAR MAN
692—THE PRINCESS & THE FROG
784—AND BABIES MAKE TEN
835—MAN BEHIND THE VOICE
887—TWINS TIMES TWO!

HARLEQUIN INTRIGUE
540—WHEN NIGHT DRAWS NEAR

Don't miss any of our special offers. Write to us at the following address for information on our newest releases.

Harlequin Reader Service
U.S.: 3010 Walden Ave., P.O. Box 1325, Buffalo, NY 14269
Canadian: P.O. Box 609, Fort Erie, Ont. L2A 5X3

Heidi and Zoë & Becca and Brianne

are happy to announce the marriage of

Heidi and Zoë's mommy

Cara Wells

to

Becca and Brianne's daddy

Ross Gifford

Please send all toys (we mean gifts!)

to the Gifford residence,

also known as "the Castle"

Chapter One

Cara Wells paused in the doorway to the kitchen and suppressed a grin. Mere feet away her twin girls were trying to scale a makeshift ladder made of their potty stool, a package of disposable training pants, and the brass handles of the drawers. Zoe, the smaller of the two, had evidently been drafted into being "top man" in the escapade, while below her, Heidi pushed at her sister's rear end in an attempt to help her crawl onto the kitchen counter.

It wasn't hard to figure out their intended goal. Only an hour ago the twins had helped Cara make a chocolate cake. Knowing the girls would be tempted to drag their fingers through the frosting, Cara had pushed it as far back into the corner as she could. But even keeping the sweet treat out of sight hadn't been enough to dissuade them from trying to get another sampling.

"Get off the counter," Cara said, softly enough to keep from startling the girls but with enough firmness to help them realize she meant business.

Immediately three-year-old Zoe twisted to look at Cara. The little girl's cornflower-blue eyes radiated an angelic innocence that belied her proximity to the cake.

"C'mon Zoe. Get the cake," Heidi urged, obviously not dissuaded by Cara's appearance.

"Down," Cara said again.

"We needa piece a cake," Heidi announced.

"That's for when we go on a picnic with Polly tomorrow afternoon." Cara's reminder had little effect so she added, *"Tomorrow."*

"No!" Heidi insisted, still pushing Zoe's rear and causing her sister to scrabble for a handhold on the slippery Formica. "We needa piece a cake now!"

Cara had to fight to keep from laughing. A part of her wanted to cave in and let them have the cake. In the six months since the state had given her legal guardianship of the children, it had been such a joy to watch them experiencing so many firsts. Each day was a conquest for them in some small way—from potty training to riding a tricycle. They took such joy from the simple things, and they'd taught Cara to look more closely at the simple beauties of the world around them. Cara liked the way they turned their faces toward the morning sun and ate ice cream with the exuberance of a gourmand.

But she also knew that it was important to set limits. Despite everything the children had been through, she couldn't spoil them rotten. After all, there was Harvard to look forward to—or perhaps a seat on the Supreme Court. If either venue proved to be part of their futures, it wouldn't do for Cara to ruin their manners in their first few months under her care.

"Can we p'ease hav'a piece?" Heidi asked, but the stamp of her foot belied the civility of her request.

"No. Now help Zoe get down."

"But, we wanna—"

Cara held up a finger in warning, and Heidi stopped her tirade in midsentence knowing already that to argue would mean a stint of "time-out" in the bedroom.

Fortunately, before Heidi could decide it might be worth the risk to press her luck, Cara was distracted by the sharp bleep of the phone. A quick glance at the ID box informed her that Polly Townsend was calling from one of the business's cell phones. Polly was a fellow partner of the Mom Squad—a mother-for-hire service that Cara and three other friends had organized less than three years earlier.

"No cake," she said again firmly, then grasped the receiver. If Polly was calling this late, there was a snag in the schedule for the evening.

It never ceased to amaze her how busy the Mom Squad was kept—especially in the evenings. Originally each of the founding partners had been searching for a way to earn a little extra money. They had never dreamed that the enterprise would bloom into a full-scale business with more requests for service than any of them could handle on their own.

"Hold on a second," Cara said into the phone. Then she looked at the twins and pointed a finger at the floor. "Down. Right now." Cara purposely used the no-nonsense tone that preceded a session of time-out, with the twins isolated in two different rooms. As usual, the thought of being separated— even for two minutes—was enough to dissuade the twins from disturbing the cake. Reluctantly Heidi stepped aside so that Cara could scoop Zoe from the counter and shoo her in the direction of the playroom.

Finally she was able to devote her attention to Polly. "Hi, Polly. What's up?"

Cara had already finished the payroll checks and stacked them neatly on the counter in preparation for delivering them to the office the following morning, so she doubted the call had anything to do with her duties as the Mom Squad's CPA.

"Melba Wilson's daughter just called, and Melba has been taken to the hospital with an apparent appendicitis attack. They're rushing her into surgery now."

"My gosh, will she be okay?"

"The surgery is fairly routine, but naturally everyone's a little worried."

"We should send someone to be with her daughter."

"I've already taken care of that. I've got Sharon on her way to the hospital now. She'll keep us posted throughout the evening and see about ordering some flowers from the hospital gift shop. Our immediate problem lies in the fact that Melba had a tending job tonight. I guess she was more concerned about canceling than she was about being hospitalized. We're stretched awfully thin. I'd go myself, but I have two job interviews to conduct later, and I haven't been able to contact the applicants. I wondered if you'd be available. You could drop the twins off at the office. They can entertain themselves in the day care room here while I do the interviews, then I'll bring them back to your place and watch them until you get back."

Accustomed to filling in for such emergencies,

Cara pulled a pad of paper closer. "Give me the address and the time I need to be there."

Polly's sigh of relief was audible. As Cara copied the information, she knew that getting to the address located on the eastern bench would be tight, but if she took a few of the back roads...

Within fifteen minutes Cara was on her way. The twins were strapped into their car seats, a bag filled with extra training pants and snacks nestled on the floor beside them. Polly was waiting for her in the parking lot of the Mom Squad offices, and it took only another few minutes to transfer the twins into her care—most of that time spent in the twins insisting on offering her numerous farewell hugs and kisses.

As she drove away and watched the girls wave to her until she turned the corner, she felt an all-too-familiar lump of emotion wedge at the base of her throat.

Zoe and Heidi had brought her so much joy— so much joy in the midst of tragedy. When Cara's brother and sister-in-law had been killed in an auto accident a year ago, Cara had received guardianship of the fraternal twins. She'd become a mother overnight, not an easy task considering the confusion and grief that all of them had suffered after the accident. But they were doing better now. Life had begun to develop a steady routine, and the anguish wasn't quite so strong, coming in sharp jabs from time to time rather than the ever-present waves.

Cara had the children to thank for that. Little Heidi, with her long blond hair and indigo eyes, was the ringleader of the pair. She could dream up more ways to get into trouble than Cara could anticipate. Zoe, on the other hand, was quiet, eager to please and a quick learner—facts that often escalated Heidi's plans for adventure. But with her carrot-colored curls and cornflower-blue eyes, she often affected an expression of angelic innocence that belied her mischievous nature.

Cara sighed, knowing that the twins had brought her more happiness than she had ever thought possible. She'd already begun formal proceedings to adopt the children—the idea having been suggested in her brother's will. Yet, if anyone had asked her only a year before if she would ever consider motherhood, she probably would have told them no. With a nasty divorce behind her, she'd been so sure she would spend the rest of her life alone. Funny the way fate could shuffle the deck and deal a hand a person had never anticipated.

Retrieving the paper with the address from her bag, Cara checked the numbers against those on the nearest street sign. She was getting close.

Making a right-hand turn, she resisted the impulse to gawk at the houses on either side of the winding road. She had entered the newer building section high on the Wasatch Bench, located to the east of Salt Lake City proper, an area reserved for homes the size of hotels. The area all but screamed of wealth and privilege.

According to Polly, their client was a lawyer. And judging by the real estate surrounding his home, he was a wildly successful one at that. Cara doubted that her yearly earnings could even pay for a building lot in the area.

In the gathering dusk, she caught a glimpse of a pair of wrought-iron gates tipped with brass. The numbers corresponded to those she'd scrawled on her planner.

"Bingo," she whispered under her breath, rolling to a stop in front of the security monitor and pressing the call button. Within seconds her summons was answered by a baritone, "Yes?"

"Hello, Mr.—" she glanced at her paper "—Mr. Gifford. I'm Cara Wells from the Mom Squad. I believe you were notified that I would be coming to watch your children tonight rather than Melba Wilson."

There was a soft, nearly imperceptible whirring sound from behind a small glass screen, and Cara resisted the urge to mug for the camera that had probably been focused on her. Ahh, the drawbacks of wealth. Constant security and the constant threat of risk. Cara would take concerned neighbors, dead bolts and peepholes on her doors over high-tech electronic surveillance equipment any day.

"Will you hold your ID up to the camera please."

Evidently Mr. Gifford was even more paranoid than most, she thought as she retrieved her wallet from her purse and held it up to the lens of the camera. She didn't think many would-be thieves or kidnappers would be riding around town in such a conspicuous van. Banking on the fact that a company car would help promote some free advertising, the Mom Squad had a small fleet of pink and blue vans complete with huge plastic booties attached to the roofs.

"Drive on in."

With no more fanfare than that the gates slid open, allowing Cara to roll onto a brick driveway laid in a herringbone pattern.

"Pretty ritzy," Cara murmured to herself. She grew even more impressed when the driveway began winding through stands of huge evergreens and oaks—the sort of transplanted foliage that had probably been fully grown and transplanted onto the lot within the last few years. Through the trees she caught a glimpse of emerald-green lawns, a pond complete with ducks and swans and...

Was that a deer? Was the place actually home to deer, or had they come down from the mountain and jumped the fence?

"I hope they had ID with them," she muttered under her breath, then laughed. No, the animals had to have been transplanted onto the grounds, as well. From the encounter she'd had at the gate, she doubted Ross Gifford would ever allow anything so untidy as unwanted deer—especially if the landscaping was any indication. As she continued to wind her way up the hill, she didn't see a stray leaf, a straggly bush or a withered flower. Everything was theme-park perfect and slightly...unreal.

"Big money," she murmured to herself. "Big, big money."

No wonder he was so careful about checking her out. That much money had to make a person paranoid, especially with young children around. Nevertheless, she couldn't help wondering why Ross didn't have a full-time nanny and a fleet of governesses. Wasn't that what wealthy people did with their children?

Realizing she was judging the man and she hadn't even met him yet, she took a deep breath. Rather than second-guess him, she should be relieved that Ross Gifford was a client of the Mom

Squad. And the fact that he was so careful with his children's welfare should bring him up a notch in her estimation. Cara was just as protective of the twins' welfare, preferring to use close friends or Mom Squad associates on those rare occasions when she needed a sitter.

Without warning the trees suddenly parted and the road curved to reveal the house. A muted "Wow" burst from her lips, and she unconsciously stopped. If she didn't know better, she would have thought she had stepped back in time. In front of her lay a modern-day castle complete with field-stone walls, mullioned windows and a pair of round turrets.

"I don't think we're in Kansas anymore," Cara whispered, then, realizing she'd slipped into her habit of talking to herself, she snapped her jaw closed. It wouldn't do to talk to herself in front of Ross Gifford. Judging by this house, he was an important client to the Mom Squad. A very, *very* important client.

Cara immediately became conscious of her worn jeans, scuffed sneakers and finger-tossed hair. Then, frantically, she looked for a place to park, knowing the van had a tiny oil leak that she hadn't seen to yet.

When it became obvious that the entire road was made of the same herringbone brick, she chose an inconspicuous spot next to a flowerbed. "Please, please don't leak," she whispered to the car, then offered the van a friendly pat on the steering wheel.

She took a moment to look in the mirror, then grimaced. The heat and her busy day had caused her hair to poke out at all angles. And even though she'd adopted a short pixie-like cut in an effort to tame the natural curls, she didn't think her hairdresser had intended it to look so...untidy.

"Damn." Then remembering she'd vowed not to talk to herself, she bit her lip and slid outside.

After slamming the door, Cara slung a duffel bag full of games, storybooks and puppet paraphernalia over her shoulder, then hurried up to the front door.

Even his door was rich and elegant, she decided with a grimace. It looked as if it had been carved from a single span of oak. Wrought-iron studs and huge rings rather than doorknobs carried out the castle theme.

A glance at her watch reassured her that she had arrived on the dot of seven. Since Ross Gifford already knew she had arrived, she debated whether or not to ring the doorbell. With her luck, he wouldn't have a doorbell. More likely he had Quasimodo sequestered in one of the towers.

When the thought caused a burst of nervous

laughter, she turned away to school her features. Almost against her will, her eyes absorbed the pristine landscaping and a house large enough to contain an orphanage. Just as she'd thought, there were deer grazing in the grass near the pond. The docile animals seemed perfectly at ease, and why wouldn't they be? They must be thinking they were in deer nirvana.

"Amazing. Absolutely amazing."

Again she pressed her lips together to keep from saying anything more out loud. She might be amazed and she might be impressed, but she had to keep her thoughts to herself. After all, she was merely the hired help for the evening. It didn't matter that the fieldstone still held a portion of the day's heat. Or that the colors of the rock made the house look as if it had stood on the site for hundreds of years. Nor was it any of her business that the absolute perfection of the scene gave Cara the willies—as if she were surveying a movie set and everything she saw was an illusion.

The sound of a throat being cleared caused her to jump and she turned.

He did have Quasimodo working for him.

No. Not Quasimodo, she quickly amended. The man who stood in front of her was far too tall, too rigid, too stiff and formal to be the bell-ringing hero of the twins' favorite cartoon. His dark suit,

crisp starched tie and gleaming black shoes be-
spoke a man who paid attention to details.

"Good evening, Miss Wells."

The British accent immediately revealed that he
wasn't the same man who'd asked to see her iden-
tification.

"I'm from the Mom Squad."

"Yes. We know."

Cara wasn't sure if the gentleman—a butler?—
was using a royal we or if he included Ross in his
statement.

She flushed when the butler looked at her car,
and his gaze flicked to the undercarriage as if he
sensed the oil that even now threatened to mar the
pristine surface of the drive.

"That will be all, Stibbs. I can handle things
from here. You'd best get to your opera before the
curtain rises."

The voice came from the shadowy interior of the
foyer. From her vantage point in the sun, Cara's
eyes couldn't adjust enough to give her a good
glimpse of the man. She had the vague impression
of height, the flash of a white shirt, but little more.

The butler nodded. "Very good, Mr. Gifford. I
do have a fondness for *La Bohème* and I would
hate to miss the overture."

With that, Stibbs disappeared into the shadows

of the house, casting one last suspicious glance at Cara's car.

Cara saw Ross's arm move as he glanced at his watch. "You've got good timing."

Cara fought the urge to curtsy like some housemaid being complimented by the lord of the manor.

At that moment Ross stepped forward, and the sun slid over his body. The light caressed dark hair still wet from a shower, craggy angular features and a lean athletic body.

Wow.

Cara wasn't usually a person who was bowled over by mere looks, but she had to admit that Ross Gifford was pleasing to the eye—even a jaundiced eye like her own. His hair was short, dark and swept back from his forehead. His features were sharp and elegant—the sort of face that graced the covers of men's magazines and fitness reports. And his eyes...

They were dark brown, piercing and infinitely bleak.

All too soon Cara was reminded that Ross Gifford was a widower with a pair of twins on his hands. His children were about the same age as hers from what she could remember Polly telling her when she'd dropped the twins off.

"I've got twins," Ross stated bluntly.

Cara noted that his hand remained on the door-jamb as if he fully expected her to turn and run.

"Yes, I know that."

Even if she'd wanted to change her mind, she couldn't have moved. His eyes held her pinned to the spot like a rabbit caught in the beam of a car's headlights. She didn't need the elegance of her surroundings to convey to her that this was a powerful man. Everything about him radiated strength and control.

"They're three."

She resisted the urge to smile. "I have twins myself, so I'm sure I'm up to the challenge."

He stared at her, and she grew infinitely self-conscious of her attire. She should have taken the time to—

To what? She had come to spend the evening tending a pair of twins. She hadn't come here to impress Ross Gifford with anything other than her mothering skills.

"Can you give me an overview of your credentials?"

Credentials? Was she going to be interviewed for a few hours' worth of work?

"What kind of education do you have?"

Cara fought the urge to offer a pithy reply. "I have a master's degree in philosophy and economics."

"I didn't think a person could actually get a job with a master's in philosophy."

Of all the nerve.

Her nerves stretched tight. "I find it immensely helpful when spending the evening with toddlers. You'd be amazed how many of them are well-versed in Descartes."

Although she'd tried to keep her tone light, there was enough of a bite to it that Ross must have realized she didn't appreciate being grilled.

His lips twitched in a self-deprecating grimace. "I hope you'll bear with me. My children can be a...challenge. I merely wanted to make sure they would be in good hands."

His shoulders shifted as if his jacket had grown too tight, and Cara wondered how many sitters had refused to help him before he'd come to the Mom Squad.

"I should have known your agency would send someone equal to the task," he said, ushering her in with a wave of his hand. "Melba is a jewel. I was sorry to hear she was rushed to the hospital. How is she?"

"In surgery now, but I'll be getting calls updating her progress throughout the evening."

Ross nodded, absorbing the information with the intensity of a man being given stock-market quotes. "I'd appreciate it if you'd keep me posted. The twins and I are very fond of Melba."

"I'll do that."

Without another word Ross turned, making his way toward a wide, sweeping staircase. "Sorry for the rush, but I've got less than an hour to get to a benefit dinner."

"No problem."

She followed him up the lushly carpeted staircase, trying her best not to look as if she were gawking. The staircase was a sweeping expanse of rich wood carved with wild animals, flowers and vines. The pale carpet underfoot looked too rich to be anything but wool.

Ross Gifford's house was immense, with high-pitched ceilings, stark white walls and pale ice-white carpets. Except for occasional splashes of color from jewel-toned pillows and the rich woodwork, everything seemed pale and colorless....

And sterile.

Again she was reminded of the fact that this man was a widower. There had been no feminine touches added to the house, no knickknacks, no family photographs, no scattered toys. If not for her job assignment, there would have been no clues that children lived here. No clues that anyone lived here at all.

Again she was filled with the sensation of having entered a showplace for the Parade of Homes design competition and the thought filled her with sadness. The house had so much promise. So much effort had been expended to make it look beautiful, but no one as yet had taken the time to make it feel like a home.

Only once did she get a hint that a family lived here. Midway down the corridor she saw a portrait of a woman with bright-red hair and piercing blue eyes.

Was this Ross's late wife?

Cara felt a twinge of sadness. How long had Ross Gifford's wife been gone? Months? Years? Were the occupants of this house still mourning her passing?

"There's a small kitchenette in the children's wing."

Wing? His children had a wing to themselves?

"The play area is located in the south turret, and their rooms are on either side. I've left my pager number, my cell number and a list of emergency contacts taped on the refrigerator. The twins have already eaten, but they may want a small snack before bedtime. Stibbs has left some fruit, milk and wheat-germ cookies."

Wheat-germ cookies? No doubt they were healthy but they sounded less than appealing.

"The children need to be in bed promptly at

8:00 p.m. Their pajamas are waiting on the counter in the bathroom. They'll need to be bathed first.''

"Of course." Ross's tone was so clipped Cara had the sensation of being briefed for battle.

"Other than that, the twins can be a handful once they realize I've left them for the evening, but they are usually well behaved. If they act out in any way, feel free to give them a paddling, but I've rarely found such a measure necessary."

Cara bit her lip to keep from saying that she was a proponent of time-out rather than spanking. It wasn't any of her business how Ross chose to discipline his children.

"If you have any problems at all, please call me. I've made arrangements to leave early, so I should be home no later than eleven."

He stopped in front of a set of double doors. Glancing at his watch, he depressed the brass handle. "I won't stay other than to quickly introduce you. If the children catch on that I'm going somewhere without them, they'll scream and cry. They handle things better if I go quickly."

"That's fine. I'm sure we'll all have a great evening together."

Ross's brow creased. "I wouldn't go at all if there were any way to get out of this event. But…"

Despite his stern manner, her heart warmed at his apparent reluctance to leave the children even for a few hours. "We'll be fine. Feel free to call if you want to check on us."

"No. That won't be necessary. I've always had good luck with the people sent by your agency." He paused, opened his mouth as if to say something, then clearly thought better of it. "Well, here goes…"

In one smooth motion he opened up the door, revealing a child's fantasy playroom on the other side.

"Becca, Brianne…this is Melba's friend, Cara. She's come to play with you for a little while. You be good for her, okay?"

In that instant a pair of children came running from the other side of the room, moving into Cara's line of sight.

And in the space of a heartbeat, the bottom dropped out of her world.

Chapter Two

Somehow Cara managed to hold on to her instinctive cry until she heard the whisper of Ross's footsteps disappear down the hall. Even so, she didn't dare move until the slam of the door was followed by the low growl of his car.

The trembling began in her extremities, moving inward until she was forced to grip the doorjamb to remain upright. Her eyes were glued to the children playing on the floor in front of her. As much as her mind rebelled against what she saw, the twins were so like her own—one a carrottop with cornflower-blue eyes; the other a strawberry-blonde with deep-indigo eyes. If not for the way the girls' haircuts were different—short and left to curl naturally—Cara would have believed that her own little girls had been brought to the house as part of an elaborate joke.

But they weren't her twins. When Ross's twins looked at her there was no recognition in their gazes. Instead they broke into hysterical cries and rushed to the window overlooking the drive.

"Daddy! Daddy, don't leave us!" one of them cried while the other pounded on the glass and sobbed.

They were "Daddy's girls." Heidi and Zoe had adored their father, as well. It had taken months for them to stop asking for Cara's brother. Now they tended to be reticent around males, probably because their world was more generally populated with women.

"Shh, shh, there's no need to cry."

Cara's instincts sent her body into autopilot. Pushing her own confusion aside, she quickly comforted the little girls, then showed them the treasures she'd brought with her in the duffel bag.

Soon the twins were assembling a floor puzzle decorated with cartoon animals. Yet, they must have sensed something in her manner because they regarded her now and again with concern and a hint of shyness.

Cara's smile was hollow and automatic. She felt numb, even though her limbs continued to tremble with shock and disbelief.

Cara's children were rarely shy. They raced up

to engage strangers in conversation as if meeting long-lost friends. But these youngsters…

No. They weren't her children. They were two completely different individuals.

Cara's stomach flip-flopped in sudden dread, and she sank into a child-size chair drawn up to a gaily painted table. In a rush she remembered the many times that her brother had teased his wife about the origins of Zoe's red hair. Patrick, her brother, had Cara's own strawberry-blond hair and indigo eyes, while his wife, Deirdre, had been a dark brunette with brown eyes.

Several times they had all joked halfheartedly that one of the twins had been switched at birth. After all, there had been a horrible blizzard the night the children were born, resulting in a blackout through much of northern Utah. Although the hospital's power had been running, due to an emergency generator, the weather had caused more than eight women to go into labor at the same time. Heidi and Zoe had been born in an ambulance en route to the hospital, and there had been rumors that another couple had given birth to twins in the hallway. Both women had been forced to wait in the corridor until rooms could become available for them and their babies could be taken the nursery.

Suddenly the family joke didn't seem nearly so funny. Was it possible that two sets of identical twins really had been switched during their stay in the hospital? Had that error created two sets of fraternal twins from what had once been two sets of identical twins? Had Deirdre accidentally brought home little Zoe, when in reality Zoe had no biological ties to the family that had raised her?

Cara's head swam at the very idea. But even as her brain tried to tell her that she was overreacting and the whole situation was a horrible joke, her heart suspected the truth. Somehow she knew her theory was right and that two sets of identical twins had been ''jumbled up'' before being sent home with their parents, creating two sets of fraternal twins. As impossible as it sounded, it was the only logical explanation for the girls.

Raking her fingers through her hair, Cara took a deep, shuddering breath. Think. *Think.*

What was she going to do now? What was she *supposed* to do now?

Why couldn't she think!

Fortunately Ross's children seemed unaware of her turmoil. Fighting her fear and panic, Cara dragged the duffel toward her and reached into one of the pockets, removing her cell phone.

Her fingers shook so badly it took three tries before Cara was able to punch in the numbers. One ring. Two.

"Come on, Polly, please," Cara whispered, her eyes still glued to Ross Gifford's twins.

They were growing unsettled by her rapt attention. Whispering to themselves, they pushed their puzzle a few feet farther away from Cara and resumed their play.

So quiet. Cara's twins were rarely quiet and rarely still. She couldn't ever remember them sitting in one place for more than a few minutes at a time, let alone quietly working on a puzzle. Becca and Brianne didn't even talk much to each other. Instead, they worked together in a way that revealed how accustomed they were to anticipating each other's needs.

Dear sweet heaven above, how could this have happened?

Cara watched them for what seemed like hours, the phone clutched against her cheek.

No, it wasn't hours. She'd only just arrived. She'd only just dialed the phone.

"Hello, this is Polly Townsend. How can I help you?"

Cara gripped the phone so hard it creaked. In the background, she could hear the happy squeals of her own twins.

Heidi and Zoe were safe. They were with Polly. This wasn't a horrible joke.

"Polly?" She opened her mouth, then realized

she didn't know what to say. Dear heaven above, she didn't even know how to explain what was wrong. All she knew was that she was suddenly afraid. Deeply, terrifyingly afraid.

"Cara?" When Cara didn't immediately respond, Polly's tone sharpened in concern. "What's wrong? Didn't you find the Gifford house?"

"Yes. Yes, I'm here now."

"Has something happened to the children? Melba told me once that they are terribly attached to their father. Sometimes they cry for a while after he leaves."

Wrong? No, nothing was wrong with the children. They were beautiful. Completely and totally perfect.

Cara sobbed. "Polly, can you get someone to take the twins home and watch them for a little while. I need you to come over as soon as you've finished there."

Polly didn't argue about finding a sitter for the twins. Instead, her voice sharpened with concern. "What's up?"

"You won't believe it unless you see it."

"'It?' Cara you're scaring me. Tell me what's wrong."

Unable to think of another way of breaking the news, Cara blurted out, "Polly, I think a mistake was made. With the twins. When they were born."

There was a pause on the other end.

"I don't understand, Cara. Are Gifford's children sick or something?"

"No." Cara bit her lip when the word emerged as another ragged sob.

"Cara, tell me what's wrong."

The sobs came swifter now and stronger. "Polly, Ross Gifford's children look like Heidi and Zoe. *Exactly* like Heidi and Zoe. I think a mistake was made on the night they were born. I think one of each set of twins was switched at the hospital and was sent home with the wrong mothers."

Her announcement was met with stunned silence. "Cara, that doesn't make any sense. Are you telling me that…"

Polly's words trailed away, and Cara quickly filled the quiet with her own words. "I'm telling you that Ross Gifford has one twin that looks like Heidi and one that looks like Zoe. And I think I've just unknowingly opened Pandora's box."

LESS THAN TWENTY MINUTES PASSED before Polly arrived, bringing with her the other partners of the Mom Squad, Bettina Wilfordson and Grace Abbington. By the time the company van pulled into the drive, Cara had bathed Ross's children and tucked them into bed. But where Heidi and Zoe would have dawdled over the tasks, Becca and

Brianne had gone to bed with a near military-like efficiency—giving Cara a clear indication that Ross Gifford was a man who liked keeping to a schedule.

Cara sank onto the couch and nibbled at her fingernail while the two women peeked in on the sleeping children. But the moment Cara caught sight of their stunned expressions, she knew that she had not overreacted.

"This is freaky," Polly whispered as she sank into a rocker.

Bettina sank cross-legged on the carpet, her skirt billowing around her. For once Bettina—who generally spoke of the effects of past lives and bad karma on everyday events—was silent.

Grace eyed Cara in concern. "So what are you going to do?"

Cara shrugged, unable to think. Her mind kept going in circles, reviewing her first glimpse of Ross's girls. She was numb and confused, her stomach knotting with a deep inexpressible fear.

"You could ignore the whole situation and continue on as before," Polly suggested.

Bettina gasped as if the cosmic forces of the universe were shuddering at the very idea. "Both sets of twins once shared the intimacy of the womb. Their psyches have unconsciously orchestrated this reunion. To separate them again would be a tragedy.''

"Let's leave the Fates out of this please,'' Grace inserted quickly before Bettina could begin elaborating on psychic bonds. "I think we would be better off focusing on the present reality of the situation.''

Cara bit her lip. "Ross Gifford has to be told.''

If Cara had expected her friends to talk her out of the idea, the silence of the room confirmed her worst fears. Yes. He would have to be told.

"How…when?'' she stammered faintly.

"The sooner the better,'' Bettina offered. "To hold on to such a secret would eat at your soul.''

"True, but I think before you start telling the man anything, you'd best think things through,'' Polly said.

"Polly is right.'' Grace sank onto the cushion next to Cara and took her hand. "You've got to look at this from every angle. And when the time comes, you'll have to tell Ross.'' She gave Cara a look of concern. "But not tonight. As much as you might want to blurt things out the minute you see him, I think you'd better consult with a lawyer before you do anything.''

"I agree,'' Polly offered. "I could call Bert

Morton and get you into his office tomorrow morning."

Cara took a deep shuddering breath. "And until then?"

The other women exchanged concerned gazes.

"We'll take over the rest of the evening for you. Why don't you go home, put your feet up—" Grace began.

"No."

Cara wasn't aware that she'd said the word aloud until the force of it surprised even her.

"No, I've got to stay and finish out the evening." Cara prayed that her friends wouldn't push her for an explanation. She wasn't sure why she wanted to stay. But she needed to be here. She needed to see Ross's children again, to study them for long minutes in the darkness of their rooms. Maybe then she would be able to sort things out for herself and bring her reeling thoughts into line.

"No, I'll stay. Ross Gifford was nervous enough about leaving his children for the evening. I won't give him any more reason for concern. From the look of things, this man has more money than God. I don't think it would be good for business to do anything to upset him."

It was easy to see from her partners' faces that

they had already come to the same conclusion but had been willing to support her needs first.

"Really," she insisted with more strength than she felt, "I'll be fine."

Eventually Cara was able to convince her friends that she wasn't in immediate danger of becoming hysterical. Even so, it was more than an hour later when the women finally climbed into the van. Cara stood at the nursery window, watching them drive away. Hoping she looked natural, she smiled and waved.

But the smile died the moment the van was lost from view.

The quiet of the house settled around her. The central air created an artificial draft that should have been pleasant but made her feel chilled instead.

Idly her gaze swept over the lawn, the artificial pond, the distant glimpse of a winding footpath and a rock bridge.

Such a beautiful home.

In the darkness Ross's estate seemed even more removed from the real world. Subdued lighting had been cleverly camouflaged to make it look as if the grounds were flooded in moonlight. From her vantage point, she could see the deer grazing beneath the trees, the ducks sleeping in the reeds, their heads tucked beneath their wings.

So serene. So beautiful. So surreal.

Once again Cara had the feeling that she had been plunged into the middle of a picture postcard or a movie set. If only she'd been given some hint of what she would find here. Maybe if she'd been more prepared...

But how could anyone be prepared for what she'd found here?

Without warning, the phone on the wall bleeped. Cara jumped, her hand flying to her chest as if to keep her heart from leaping free.

Taking a deep breath, she lifted the receiver. "This is the Gifford residence, may I help you?"

"This is Ross. I'm on my way home now."

There was a pause, and Cara wondered how she was supposed to respond to his blunt announcement.

Yes, sir?

Whatever you say, sir?

"Very good, Mr. Gifford." Damn. That sounded like something the stuffy Stibbs might say.

"How have things gone?"

Again, her stomach flip-flopped. Then, with the realization that she would soon be confronting Ross face-to-face, she fought a flash of dizziness.

What was she going to do?

What was she going to say?

"Miss Wells?"

"Th-the children were wonderful. They're sleeping soundly right now."

"Did you have any problems when I left?"

Such as her well-ordered existence tumbling down around her ears?

"No. They were fine."

There was a beat of silence.

"Really?"

"Yes." Then she quickly amended, "They cried a bit when they realized you were gone, but I was able to divert their attention with a puzzle."

"I'm impressed. Even Melba has a hard time getting them to sleep. They tend to get nervous and whiney unless I'm home."

"Then they must have been very tired because they didn't put up a fuss."

"And how is Melba?"

Cara had been so embroiled in her own concerns, she'd forgotten to phone Ross with an update as she'd promised. "She's out of surgery and doing well."

"That's good news. I'll see you in five minutes."

A click in her ear let her know the call had been terminated, and for some unaccountable reason she was miffed at the sudden dismissal. He'd hung up without so much as a word of farewell as if she were...

An employee.

But wasn't that exactly what she was? In fact, she couldn't even lay claim to that much of a role in his life. She was a "temp" of sorts who had been hired to fill in for a few hours. And now instead of slipping out of his life as easily as she'd drifted in, she was here...

To stay?

No. Despite what she had discovered, she wasn't about to become a part of Ross Gifford's life. They would sort out this mess and she would go back to her routine.

But even as she insisted such a thing to herself, she instinctively knew that she was underestimating the effects of the newfound knowledge. No matter what happened from this point on, she and Ross would be forever linked, due to an error made by a hospital employee years earlier.

Her nerves stretched even tighter, threatening to snap. More than anything she wanted to go home, curl up in the rocking chair in her children's bedroom and surround herself in all that was comfortable and familiar. But before she would be able to do that, she would have to "make small talk"

with an important client. She would have to sum-
mon all of her inner strength so that she gave no
hint of the turmoil roiling just below the surface
of her artificial calm.

Five minutes. She had five minutes before…

Before what? She had already decided to take
Grace's advice. There would be no late-night con-
fessions. As long as she kept her cool, Ross Gifford would remain blissfully ignorant of the
hospital's mistake. Until then…

Until then nothing would happen. Nothing whatsoever.

But as she pressed a trembling hand to her chest,
she realized a part of her wasn't completely convinced. Her heart was racing as if she'd run a mile.

The whir of the garage-door opener disturbed
the stillness of the house. Her heart leaped in her
breast, then seemed to sink into the pit of her stomach.

Keep your cool. Just keep your cool.

Suddenly galvanized into action, she hurried
around the nursery, repacking her supplies and
stuffing them willy-nilly into the duffel bag. As
soon as she'd said her goodbyes, she would go
home. Once there, she could reassure herself that
her own twins were safe and well and tucked into
their own beds.

"It's quiet."

Ross's voice caused Cara to jump, and she whirled to face him, her pulse racing more than ever.

"You startled me," she gasped, then wished she'd remained silent when her voice sounded slightly frantic even to her own ears.

A crease appeared between Ross's brow, but other than that, he didn't seem overly concerned by her reaction. "Sorry. I thought you would have heard the car."

She caught his gaze only momentarily, then returned her attention to the toys.

"How was your evening?"

"Fine."

So much for chitchat. Ross turned away from her, moving from one bedroom to the next checking on the girls. She waited in tense expectation as if simply by seeing the twins he would guess that something was wrong.

"They look no worse for wear."

Cara didn't know how she was supposed to react to such a remark. Insulted, probably. He made it sound as if he'd been expecting the worst.

"They're beautiful children." Just as her own children were beautiful. "You must be very proud." Just as Cara was inestimably proud.

She bit her lip. Maybe she shouldn't have said anything. Had a note of fondness crept into her tone? One that she felt for her own children?

To her dismay she realized that all of the toys were packed away and the room was tidy. As her heart seemed to sink into her stomach, Cara realized that she had no other option but to look him square in the eye.

She could only pray that he wouldn't look at her and know her life had been shaken to its very core.

Chapter Three

Cara felt a jolt of something akin to electricity shoot through her system when their gazes locked, but she quickly dismissed the reaction, knowing that her nerves were strung as tightly as a tennis racket.

"I'm impressed at the way you were able to get them to bed so easily," Ross said. "Usually the girls are very fractious with a new sitter."

Fractious. Cara was sure that she'd never heard anyone use the word in a sentence before. But she shouldn't be so surprised. Ross Gifford was obviously very educated and sophisticated. He probably said and did a lot of things that were beyond her daily realm. He belonged to the same world as her ex-husband. One filled with pomp and ceremony and an overwhelming interest in appearances. Hadn't she learned that lesson more than once where Elliot was concerned? He'd been so consumed with the need to look and speak the part of a cultured man of the world that she hadn't known what a bastard she'd married until she'd discovered that he was spending most of his time with another woman.

"In fact, I usually have problems with the girls even if I leave them with someone with whom they are acquainted.

She shrugged. "Surely they've done well with Melba. She must be used to their routines by now."

"Yes, but even when she visits, they won't go to bed as easily as you've said. If Melba manages to convince them to sleep, they wake up as soon as they hear the car in the garage."

"Like I said, maybe they were tired out. They didn't give me a bit of trouble all night."

One of his brows lifted. "Really?"

He seemed so surprised that Cara asked, "Were you expecting a riot?"

He took a deep breath and seemed to consider his words. "Frankly, judging from past baby-sitting experiences, I was expecting crying, screaming and tantrums that would continue unabated for hours on end."

Cara couldn't help quipping, "From the children or their baby-sitter?"

His lips tugged in the faintest hint of a grin—one that made her breath catch in her throat.

"Both, actually."

"Why? They seem like perfect angels to me."

"Then they were definitely on their best behavior." His eyes narrowed and she felt him studying her. Her heart knocked against her ribs when she wondered what he saw there. Could some hint of the shock she'd experienced still linger on her face despite her efforts to remain calm?

Ross's gaze was intent but not suspicious. Instead, he looked at her the way that...

The way that a man looked at a woman when he was interested.

No. Cara immediately pushed the idea aside. She was overreacting, that was all. Her thoughts and her emotions were off-kilter. She was confused and unsettled.

So why was she lingering when the time had come for her to leave?

"I...I should go now," she said. "I'm sure you've had a long day."

Ross offered her a curt nod and tugged at his tie, making her overtly conscious of the lean strength of his fingers and the slight dusting of hair on the backs of his hands.

"It has been a long day, but I tend to get a little

wired after one of these evenings. Will you join me for some coffee?''

No. Absolutely not.

But even as the inner voice warned her, she was so startled by the invitation that she found herself saying instead, ''Sure.''

''Good.''

He dragged the tie free from his collar and released the top button at his collar. Then a second button. A third.

Cara found her gaze latching on to that vee of flesh exposed against the crisp white of his dress shirt. He really was a good-looking man.

Perhaps a little too good-looking.

Cara didn't trust that quality in a man, either. Elliot had been male-model handsome, but she had discovered soon enough that the outer beauty camouflaged a weak character.

So why, after vowing to herself that she wouldn't be caught in the same trap again, did she feel the faint stirrings of attraction?

No. Absolutely not! She didn't find him in the least bit attractive.

But even as she insisted as much to herself, a tingling awareness spread through her veins as he extended a hand toward her.

''I'll carry that for you.''

Unconsciously Cara clutched the duffel bag

even more securely—as if it were a shield to protect her from…

From what?

There was nothing about Ross Gifford's appearance or manner to make her feel threatened. In fact, the sadness that cloaked his features made her feel as if she should be doing something for him rather than for herself.

But as she admitted the twinge of concern, she knew that she couldn't give in to such emotions. She couldn't dwell on her physical reaction to the man. She couldn't afford that luxury. Such emotions would simply complicate the situation—and heaven only knew her current predicament was already untenable.

Since Ross was still waiting, she reluctantly handed him the duffel bag, all the while wishing she hadn't agreed to stay for coffee. She was playing with fire and had no doubts that she would get burned.

Ross led the way through the big, silent house, offering Cara glimpses of rooms that were lushly decorated but curiously devoid of color. At long last they reached the kitchen with its white cabinets, pale tile and pale marble counters.

Who was responsible for the absence of color in the house? Was it a designer's decision or had Ross made the choice?

"Have a seat," Ross said, gesturing to a pair of stools drawn up to an ornate center island.

"Decaf or regular coffee," he asked.

"Decaf."

Ross shrugged out of his jacket and laid it over a chair. As he moved to prepare the coffee, her gaze immediately latched on to the crisp starched shirt. The long evening had rumpled the fabric at his back.

Cara didn't know why, but the sight was oddly intimate and exciting. Inexplicably Cara found herself wondering who starched those shirts, ironed them and hung them in his closet. A cleaning service? A housekeeper? Stibbs?

Or a woman who had already begun to heal his grieving heart?

"So...you're a regular with the Mom Squad?"

She jumped, her gaze bouncing away from Ross when he suddenly turned and caught her staring.

"Yes. I'm one of the founding partners."

One of his brows rose. He had dark eyes, expressive eyes, and even when he was apparently relaxed, they were filled with such a poignant sadness that Cara wanted to take him into her arms.

Stop it! The man isn't a wounded bird to bring home and keep warm in a shoebox.

But hadn't she always had a soft heart for wounded animals and strays? Isn't that how she'd found herself marrying her first husband? She'd met Elliot when he'd been on the rebound from a three-year relationship, and she'd been determined to make him smile again.

Little had she known…

"If you're one of the founding partners of the Mom Squad, why are you still taking baby-sitting jobs?" Ross asked, bringing her thoughts abruptly back to the present.

Not wanting to wallow in the past, Cara concentrated on the man in front of her instead. There was a simple grace to his movements as he measured the grounds and water into a gleaming stainless steel coffeemaker. Then he reached into an overhead cabinet for mugs. She watched transfixed as his shirt pulled taut, revealing the muscular outlines of his back.

Ross Gifford was certainly fit. Healthy.

Beautiful.

Cara forced herself to look away. "I'm the company accountant, but I fill in when there's a need."

"Your husband doesn't object to the late nights?"

"My husband?" Briefly, she thought of Elliot. Elliot definitely would have complained about the late hours if she hadn't left their relationship long before the Mom Squad was formed.

"You mentioned you had twin girls."

She stared at him blankly, her pulse knocking at her throat, then realized that she had offered the information before she'd seen Ross's children.

He doesn't know anything. Keep your cool.

"Yes. They're...three." The information was offered carefully, slowly. She watched Ross for a hint of unease but there was no reaction—not that she should have expected one.

"Boys or girls?"

Her heart thumped again.

"Girls."

"Twins can be a handful, can't they?"

She nodded. "They're a challenge at times, especially for a new mom."

He leaned his hips against the counter. "New mom?"

"The children are...were my brother's, actually. But he was killed a year ago. Since then the girls have lived with me."

For a moment the room thrummed with the reminder that life could be changed in a heartbeat. Then Ross straightened and reached into cupboards again, removing sugar and spoons, then grabbed a carton of cream from the refrigerator.

"So you're a single mom?"

Now why did it seem as if he'd put a slight emphasis on the word *single?*

"Yes. I was married once. Briefly." *Enough. He*

doesn't need to know any of this. He's merely making polite conversation.

"What happened?"

She shrugged, hoping that she didn't appear as vulnerable and exposed as she felt.

"My husband...my ex-husband and I grew apart."

The simple reply was an understatement. Elliot Wells was charismatic, charming and driven. As CEO of a fast-track marketing firm, he had dazzled her with his sophistication and discipline. He'd wooed her with wildly romantic rendezvous, expensive gifts and just the right amount of flattery and adoration.

But soon after marrying him, Cara had discovered that Elliot was a control freak who had married her because she made an excellent "trophy wife." She was beautiful and biddable—the perfect requirements in Elliot's estimation. Little had she known that Elliot kept a mistress on the side— someone who was passionate and spontaneous but not an acceptable business hostess.

"I take it the divorce wasn't amicable."

She grimaced. "How can you tell?"

"The long silence speaks volumes, I'm afraid."

"As I said, we grew apart. Soon we didn't have the same goals for the future. Elliot wanted to make as much money in as little time as possible."

"And what did you want?"

She didn't even have to think. "Happiness."

"Have you found it?"

Her smile was quick. "Yes. In a pair of irascible twins."

Ross filled their mugs with coffee and handed her one. Then he took a seat on the nearest stool.

She was immediately conscious of the firm musculature revealed beneath the fine fabric of his trousers. She could all but feel the heat of his body seeping into her own.

Cara took a quick sip of coffee, then gulped and began to cough when it burned her tongue.

"It's hot," Ross offered too late.

She laughed, then coughed again. Ross smiled—briefly, ever so briefly, but long enough for his amusement to momentarily chase away the shadows in his eyes. And at that moment she saw a glimpse of just how devastatingly handsome this man could be when he wasn't so sober.

Setting his own mug on the counter, Ross pounded her obligingly on the back. In an instant the frivolity of the moment faded away leaving a potent awareness.

Without warning, Cara felt his fingers still against her spine, then spread wide over her shoulders. Before she could fully prepare herself, there was a slight pressure against her spine and he drew her irresistibly toward him.

Inch by inch. Heartbeat by heartbeat. Closer and closer until...

Cara knew he meant to kiss her, and her brain whispered a word of warning. But suddenly she didn't care. She didn't care that she was opening herself to heartache. She didn't care that her relationship to this man was doomed from the very beginning. All that mattered was this instant.

This kiss.

Ross closed the last few inches with aching slowness. At long last his mouth settled upon hers, questioningly at first, then with greater strength and assurance.

He feels so good, so strong, so...male.

In an instant her hunger ignited in a flashpoint of need. Ross returned in kind until any emotional restraints they might offer were lost as they clung to each other, passion flaring white-hot and unexpected.

Cara's arms swept around his shoulders, and she leaned close to the man, allowing him to press her close to the hard strength of his chest. A part of her knew that what she was doing was dangerous. She was kissing a man who might someday make a claim on one of the twins. But with his arms around her, she couldn't think that far. She was consumed with a need like nothing she had ever felt before. And the pleasure…sweet heaven, she had never felt such pleasure in Elliot's arms! Ross knew just how to hold her, caress her, kiss her, to make her feel cherished and desirable, beautiful and seductive.

And she hadn't felt that way in a very long time. Not since returning home early from a dinner with her friends to discover her husband was making love to another woman in the same bed that she'd shared with him only the night before.

Suddenly starving for air, the two of them broke apart. But the need thrummed between them even more potently, swamping whatever restraints they might have cared to impose.

Cara had never experienced anything like this before. She was normally so careful around men. After her divorce she'd rarely dated—and that had been by her own choosing.

But as she looked into the dark depths of Ross's eyes, she was lost again. When he reached for her, she didn't resist. This time their embrace was slow and lingering and infinitely sensual. Her hands spread wide over his back, sweeping low to tug the hem of his shirt free, then explore the bare flesh beneath. His hissing inhalation told her that he must have felt the same jolt of electricity that coursed through her fingertips the moment she'd grazed the sensitive skin. The very thought that she could incite such a reaction filled her with an even hotter passion.

"We've got to stop," he rasped against her throat. But rather than end the embrace, he trailed his tongue along a particularly sensitive nerve, causing her to gasp.

This time it was her turn to pull him to her for a kiss. Again, she was struck by the differences between Elliot and this near stranger. Elliot had been a sloppy kisser—too wet, too intrusive. But Ross...

Ross knew just when to advance, to retreat. When to stroke, when to tease.

She moaned deep in her throat, slowly losing her touch with reality. There was only this man. This kiss.

Without warning, a high-pitched bleeping noise split the silence. The two of them sprang apart as if a shot had rung through the room.

It took a moment for Cara to realize the sound was coming from her duffel bag.

"My phone," she gasped, dodging toward the bag. The noise increased as she removed the receiver from its pocket and punched the send button.

"Yes?"

Did she really sound that breathless? That out of control?

"Cara? Are you all right?"

Polly.

"Yes. Yes, I'm fine."

"You sound strained. Did something happen when Ross came home? Did he find out there was a problem?"

Cara automatically smoothed her hair, even though Polly couldn't possibly see her. "No. I'm…I'm still here."

"What's the matter?"

"Nothing, I just stayed for coffee, that's all."

"You did *what?*" Polly's tone was incredulous.

Suddenly Cara felt like a teenager who'd broken curfew. If Polly was this shocked that Cara had stayed for coffee, imagine her reaction if she knew the full details. "I should be home in about ten minutes."

"You're sure you're okay?"

"Yes, yes. I'll see you soon."

Cara terminated the call before Polly's concern communicated itself through the slight noises that Ross must be able to hear.

"Trouble?"

"No. Just the…ah…baby-sitter."

"You hired a baby-sitter so that you could come tend my kids?"

"Not exactly. One of my partners was watching them. She thought I would be back by now."

"Ah."

The silence pulsed between them, fraught with the memories of the passionate embrace they had just shared.

Staring at Ross, she saw her own discomfort reflected in his eyes. They had just shared a terribly intimate embrace and yet they were strangers. Complete and total strangers?

So what did they do now? What were they supposed to say to each other?

Cara was the first to speak. "I, uh... I've got to go."

So why wasn't she moving?

Ross nodded, his eyes never leaving her face. "Sure. I understand. After all, I know all about getting back in time to relieve the sitter." His lips twitched in something akin to chagrin. The expression had a little-boy charm that tugged at her heart. Before grief had tainted this man's expression, he must have been devastating. If a slight twitch of his lips had the ability to knock at her defenses, what would a full-blown smile do?

Just as quickly as the smile had appeared, it disappeared again. He grew instantly serious, and she regretted the hint of gentleness. Before she could reconcile herself to the transformation, Ross was once again the epitome of a powerful businessman. In a heartbeat, the approachable person who had kissed her so spontaneously disappeared so completely, she might have imagined the interlude if her body didn't still tremble with the aftereffects.

"Listen…" Ross slid a hand into the pocket of his trousers and stared down at the toe of his shoe. "I want you to know I don't usually go around… kissing my baby-sitters."

She hitched the duffel bag over her shoulder, her own cheeks growing hot. "Of course not, and I don't—"

"No, you wouldn't."

Again the room shimmered in a heavy silence.

"Well," she whispered. "I've got to go."

He gently lifted the bag, relieving her of its weight. "I'll walk you to your car."

As they made their way to the front of the house, Cara was even more conscious of Ross beside her—and the awareness frightened her.

What was wrong with her? She'd sworn off men after Elliot. What was it about this particular male that urged her to abandon all those heartfelt promises? Had she totally lost her mind? Why couldn't she remember everything that was at stake as soon as Ross discovered the truth about their children?

Needing something to distract her from her troubling behavior and the uncertainty of the future,

Cara asked, "So what do you do, Ross? For a living, I mean."

"I'm a lawyer."

She stumbled, then quickly righted herself. A lawyer. The sick fear returned with the strength of a blow to the stomach.

A lawyer! Becca and Brianne's father was a lawyer?

What had she done? Why, oh, why hadn't she listened to her first instincts and left this house as soon as Ross arrived?

Her eyes swept over the interior of Ross's house—the hand-carved wood, the expensive furnishings and the framed art that she had supposed were prints but she now suspected were originals.

"What, uh, what kind of law?"

Please let him be a tax lawyer or a patent lawyer. Something innocuous and not nearly so threatening.

"I specialize in family law. Divorces, custody suits. Things like that."

Cara nearly lost her footing on the front stoop, then quickly righted herself before Ross could touch her again.

Wouldn't she ever learn? When would she realize that she was invariably attracted to the wrong sorts of men? She had inner radar that seemed to attract those who were in a position to hurt her.

But none of the men she'd been attracted to in the past had the kind of power that Ross unwittingly held. Not even Elliot. Elliot had once had the power to hurt and humiliate her. But Ross...

Ross could threaten her role in her children's lives.

Cara went hot then cold. By surrendering to temptation and kissing Ross she had complicated matters between them even further. No matter what she did from this moment on, the memory of their embrace would linger. She had allowed a personal element to taint a relationship that should have remained...

What? Professional? Distant? How could either of those things be possible when it was apparent that their futures would be irretrievably linked through their children?

Cara numbly made her way to the van, but as she was about to climb inside, Ross touched her arm.

"I'd like to call you."

She froze, knowing that they would be seeing each other on an entirely different footing than the one Ross was envisioning. Steeling herself, she tried to forget the sweet passion they'd shared in the kitchen and focus instead on her earlier misgivings about the man. After all, nothing had changed. Ross was still a man to be avoided. His wealth, his occupation and his grim sense of control frightened her. He was altogether too much like her ex-husband—too driven and goal oriented. Too powerful.

And he was a lawyer.

She swallowed against a wave of panic as an even newer fear rose to the surface. Her adoption of the twins wasn't finalized. Could the mix-up with the twins delay the adoption? And what if Ross decided to make claims on his biological child? Could Ross take one of the twins away from her? He certainly had the connections, money and legal know-how to do so if he wished.

"I've got to go."

She quickly climbed into the car, ignoring the flare of disappointment that glimmered in Ross's eyes before it was hidden by a blank mask.

"Of course. I guess the Mom Squad will bill me as usual?"

"Yes."

He nodded, grimaced, then backed away. "Good night, then."

He shut the door with a secure snap, then backed away so that she could maneuver the van out of the driveway.

But as the security gates rolled shut behind her, she felt as if she'd left something behind her...and the feeling wasn't entirely due to the twins.

Chapter Four

Ross stood for long moments watching the lights of Cara's car as they flickered through the trees, then disappeared altogether. Several seconds later he sighed and returned to the house.

Habit took over the moment the door was closed. He set the alarm in the foyer, turned off the lights and made his way upstairs. He'd had an exhausting day—court, two consultations and the benefit dinner. But even though he'd vowed to return home and go straight to bed rather than work until the wee hours of the morning, he hadn't. Instead, he had been more interested in indulging in the company of a woman like Cara than getting some much-needed rest.

A woman like Cara.

He couldn't remember the last time he'd been near someone so beautiful and so completely unaware of her own attractiveness. She had the subtle innocence of the "girl next door" combined with an innate sensuality. Her features were exotic, her coloring dramatic. If it weren't for the way she all but radiated "do not touch" he might have been tempted to...

His thoughts skidded to a halt, and he felt a pang of something that felt very much like guilt. Climbing the stairs, he tried his best to shake off the sensation. But even though his head told him that Nancy had been gone for nearly two years and he was more than free to look at another woman if he wanted, his heart was not so easily convinced.

Ross knew his friends and associates were completely in favor of his moving on. More than once they'd urged him to find a woman to share his life and ease the challenges of caring for the children alone. He'd heard all of the arguments about the twins needing a mother and him needing a companion. But it wasn't as easy to move on with his life as others might suppose. He and Nancy had known each other since the first grade. They'd been high school sweethearts, attended college and married soon after Ross finished his undergraduate work.

And he missed her. Dear heaven, how he missed her.

So why was he remembering another woman's

perfume and the silky texture of her skin? Why was Cara's the face he was thinking of as he undressed and prepared for bed?

Ross grunted self-deprecatingly at his own weakness. He was merely starved for feminine companionship, that was all. Any other woman would have affected him in much the same way, given the same circumstances.

The moment the thought appeared, he dismissed it as unfair. As much as he might want to discount what had happened tonight, he couldn't. Somehow, some way this woman had cracked the hard shell of ice that had encased his emotions since Nancy's death. As much as he might want to step back into the numb cocoon that had encased him for the past two years, the time had come to move on.

Nevertheless, even as he gave himself permission to go in search of companionship, to find a wife for himself and a mother for his children, he knew it wouldn't be that easy. He might succumb to his physical needs and initiate a physical relationship, but there would be no emotional ties to bind him. That part of his personality had died with his wife.

No. He would need to find a woman who could take him for what he was—scarred and imperfect. He was a man who could offer a woman a good life, a healthy bank account and an instant family.

But that was all. That was all he had left in him to give.

So why did that leave him feeling hollow? And restless?

And why couldn't he seem to forget the taste and feel of a woman who had all but run away from him only hours before?

"MR. MORTON IS STILL in conference, but he'll be right with you, Miss Wells. If you'll have a seat, I'll let him know you're waiting."

"Thank you."

Cara gripped the strap of her bag more tightly and moved into the elegant decor of the law offices' reception area. Sitting with her back to the bright light streaming through the main door, she ignored the stack of glossy magazines spread out on the table in front of her and reached into her purse instead.

Removing the two photographs, she stared at them again. Why was the sight of two sets of twins still so shocking? Why couldn't she bring herself to believe in the evidence of her own eyes?

Her thumb lovingly traced the small photograph taken of Heidi and Zoe at a portrait studio in a nearby department store. Then she looked at the Polaroid photograph that she had removed from Ross Gifford's file at the Mom Squad offices. Two sets of identical twins. Two. How had they been switched? How? Even with the confusion of the blizzard, there was no excuse for the hospital's having made such a mistake. None whatsoever.

But railing against the Fates wouldn't change the predicament she found herself in now. And there was no use fretting over things she couldn't change. The facts would still remain.

A pair of twins had been switched.

And their father had awakened a hunger in her that she was having a hard time ignoring.

No. She couldn't think about that right now. She had to keep her mind on the twins and on her options for the future. She couldn't afford to let her thoughts wander to those heady moments in Ross Gifford's arms.

"Cara?"

She froze, wondering if she was beginning to lose her mind. Now, instead of just thinking about the man, she was hearing him, too.

But when she turned, she found Ross striding through the main doors, a hint of surprise softening the granite-hard angles of his features. His gaze was intent and so obviously male that Cara felt flustered. For a moment the potent awareness in his eyes had chased away some of somberness. If he weren't so obviously in mourning, Ross Gifford would be a devastating man.

And if that were the case, how would she have the will to resist him?

She grimaced at her own inability to push aside her attraction to Ross Gifford. Why couldn't she remember that this man was a threat to everything she held dear? Why couldn't she focus on the fact that he held her future in the palm of his hand and he didn't even know it? Wasn't she in enough trouble already?

Yes. More than she could ever imagine.

So why was a tiny voice urging her to revel in this man's attention? Why was it whispering that she might have sworn off marriage, but she hadn't sworn off sex?

Shocked at her own inner musings, Cara forced herself to ignore the heat that immediately blossomed within her.

She wouldn't give in to the neediness she felt. She mustn't give in.

"Ross," she breathed, stuffing the pictures back into her bag.

"Do you have business with Walter Gibbons?" He gestured toward the inner offices with a hitch of his shoulder.

"No. W-with Bert Morton." She laughed, then wished she hadn't when it sounded too bright and too false. "Nothing serious, just some legal advice for...for the Mom Squad."

"Really? I wish you'd let me know. I would be more than happy to consult with the Mom Squad pro bono. Heaven only knows that your company has bailed me out of a jam a time or two."

"I...I—" What was she supposed to say? That there was no way she would ever ask for his help because he was part of the problem?

Her gaze bounced from the inner office doors to the receptionist. But the woman was talking on the telephone and didn't intercept Cara's silent plea for help.

Again she was filled with a wave of panic. She shouldn't have come today. If Ross found out that she'd been here, that she'd gone immediately to a lawyer rather than approaching him with her discovery...

She had to get out of here. Now.

Cara jumped to her feet. To her horror her hands lost their grip on her purse and it fell to the ground, spilling its contents all over the plush forest-green carpet.

Her face flamed, and she scrambled to gather the scattered flotsam of her busy life—cosmetics, wipes, odd barrettes and Mom Squad correspondence. But before she could react, Ross had knelt beside her. Too late, she watched as he scooped up the photographs that had fluttered to a spot out of her reach.

An instinctive cry burst from her lips as he looked down at the two prints. Two sets of twins.

"What's this?"

His brow furrowed and he looked at Cara with patent confusion, his mind not yet grasping the import of what he was seeing.

"Why do you have photographs of Becca and Brianne in your purse?"

Her throat seemed to squeeze shut, allowing no sound to escape. Then, panicking, she snatched the photographs from his lax grip and stood.

"I've got to go," she half sobbed, tears gathering behind her eyes. It was only a matter of time now. Then he would know everything and any hope of seeing his eyes grow warm would be gone.

Dear, sweet heaven, why did such a prospect fill her with an overwhelming regret?

A CHILL WAVE OF ALARM flooded Ross's system. His heart thudded sickly in his breast as he watched Cara rush toward the double doors, but he was rooted to the spot.

This woman was carrying photographs of his twins. How? Why?

Still not fully understanding the situation, Ross rushed to follow her, knowing only that he needed an explanation. But he arrived just as the double doors to the elevator closed, shutting out all but one quick glance of her distraught expression.

It was the brief flash of fear in her eyes that spurred him on. Racing to the emergency exit, he took the stairs two at a time, arriving in the lobby just as Cara tried to dodge through the outer doors.

Knowing only that he had to stop her, he snagged her elbow, pulling her tightly against him. But when her instinctive cries began to capture the attention of the other patrons, he quickly pulled her down the corridor next to the elevators, into an empty conference room and closed the door.

Immediately she wrenched free and put the width of the table between them. Breathing hard, Ross said, "I think you owe me an explanation. Why do you have photographs of my children in your purse?"

She gazed at him as if he were a monster, her eyes brimming with tears.

"I...I—"

"You are from the Mom Squad, aren't you?" Anger swelled within him, then fear. He was always so careful with his children. In his line of work he'd learned that wealth and prestige carried its own price tag, and he would stop at nothing to ensure the safety of the twins.

"Mr. Gifford? Miss Wells? Is something wrong?"

Before Ross knew what was happening, the door whipped opened and the receptionist from upstairs stepped inside.

Ross turned to reassure the woman, but in that scant moment when Ross's attention was diverted, Cara slipped past the woman and ran outside.

Again Ross tried to follow her, but by the time he reached the sidewalk, he saw her climbing into a candy-apple-red Volkswagen Beetle. Tires squealed as she backed out, and he barely had time to note her vanity plates. But even the whimsical WHEEE couldn't allay his concerns.

"Mr. Gifford?"

The receptionist had followed him outside, so Ross waved aside her concern. "I've got to get home, Bernice. Family emergency. Can you re-schedule my appointments for me?"

"Of course."

"Thanks."

Without explaining himself further, Ross loped toward his car, retrieving his cell phone from his pocket as he ran. Punching the speed dial that would connect him with his office, he waited for his secretary to answer.

"Marci, do you still have that connection with the DMV? I need an address fast."

"What have you got for me?"

"A vanity plate."

"Go ahead."

"It's WHEEE."

There was a pause. "Excuse me?"

"W-H-E-E-E."

"Gotcha."

"Call me back as soon as you've got it."

Less than ten minutes had elapsed before his phone rang again. In that time, Ross had aimlessly circled the nearby streets in his car, hoping to catch a glimpse of a candy-apple-red Volkswagen. With each second that passed, he grew more and more convinced that something was going on here, something he should be grasping about the entire situation. But what?

He'd known Cara for less than a day, yet he felt drawn to her in a way he had thought was purely physical. But was there something else between them that he was refusing to see?

Damn it all to hell. He shouldn't have kissed the woman. He shouldn't have given in to the reawakening of his physical hungers. By focusing on himself rather than his children, he had allowed his guard to drop. He couldn't afford to make such a mistake. He had too much to worry about with his life as it was. He didn't need to open himself up to more—

More what? Pleasure or pain?

The phone beeped and he grabbed it in mid-ring.

"Her name is Cara Wells. If you've got a pen, I'll give you her address."

Within minutes Ross found himself on the stoop of a quaint bungalow located in the Avenues. Steeling himself against everything but the fury that had begun to build within him, he pressed his finger against the bell and kept it there.

But he didn't have long to wait. Almost instantly the door creaked open and he found himself staring down at a familiar pair of faces—one a brilliant carrot top, the other a strawberry blonde.

"Becca? Brianne? What the—"

The anger within him flared, then suddenly turned to ice as Cara stepped into the doorway behind the children. In an instant he was struck by the disparity of the scene in front of him. Becca and Brianne? The faces were so familiar to him, so dear, so earnest....

But there was no recognition in their features. And the hair, the clothes...

"Ross, I'd like you to meet my children," Cara said, her voice low and filled with resignation. "Heidi, Zoe, this is Mr. Gifford. Believe it or not, he has a pair of twin daughters that look just like you."

THE MAN IN FRONT OF HER grew pale, and knowing from her own experience the swirl of confusion and disbelief that was robbing the color from his skin, Cara waved wide with her hand.

"Come in and take a seat. The time has come for us to have a talk."

He moved slowly, woodenly, with none of the usual grace that she'd begun to expect from him. All the while his gaze clung to Heidi and Zoe.

"But they're—"

"Yes, I know. Please. Sit down."

Briefly he tore his eyes away from the children. She saw the way he looked around him, but sensed he only absorbed a small portion of what he saw.

Looking at the room with new eyes, Cara winced. Toys littered the floor, and a pile of books had been left on the couch. The room was small, the furnishings a hodgepodge of antiques and flea market finds.

Briefly Cara wondered what Ross was thinking, if he was comparing his sumptuous castle to her own simple home. Polly had once said that Cara's bungalow looked like a Laura Ashley catalog had exploded. She loved pastel colors, chintz, English roses and a rich combination of textures. But she also loved comfort. Her favorite books were always at hand and her shoes were invariably kicked off at the door. And since the children played primarily in the living room, there was hardly a time when everything was in its place.

She shifted nervously. "Excuse the mess. The children have been playing in here."

There was no separate nursery or play area. Cara's home was a compact, one-story bungalow that had been built sometime during the depression. Cara had immediately been attracted to its charm and craftsmanship so the size hadn't been an issue. But she supposed that her entire house could fit into the nursery area devoted to Ross's children.

"How long have you known?" His voice was low and gruff.

"Only since seeing your twins yesterday."

"Did Melba say something? Was she really ill?"

"Yes. I can assure you that my appearance as your sitter was purely by chance. I only fill in when there's an emergency. As for Melba, she's never seen my children so she would have no reason to think anything was wrong. Melba works out of her home for the most part, so I was alone during those few times we met face-to-face."

Again Ross stared at her children. Cara remained silent, knowing that he would need some time to absorb the truth of what he was seeing.

The twins ran to her side, sensing the tension in the air.

"What's wrong with him, Mama?" Zoe asked, tugging at Cara's skirt.

"Nothing, sweetie. He's just thinking, that's all."

Heidi sniffed, clearly unimpressed with the stranger. "He looks like he needs a nap. Make him go home. I don' like him. He's starin' an' we're not supposed t' stare."

"Shh," Cara said, offering both girls a quick kiss. "Go play with your toys for a little while. Mr. Gifford and I need to talk."

Zoe rose on tiptoe to whisper in Cara's ear. "Can we have a cookie?"

"One each. Take them off the plate. The cookies on the baking sheet are still hot."

Ross's presence was quickly forgotten as the little girls thundered into the kitchen, giggling and jabbering to each other.

"They're so..."

"Like your little girls?" Cara finished.

He nodded.

"I couldn't believe it myself last night. I thought it was a horrible joke."

He rubbed his hand over his mouth, staring at a point in midair. "How could this be?"

Cara shrugged. "As near as I've been able to piece together, the twins must have been switched at the hospital."

He was so obviously stunned, that Cara gave him a few moments of silence to think about that long-ago night when his children were born. Although she knew it would have been wiser to speak with her lawyer first, she couldn't deny that she was secretly relieved that the truth was out.

"I've been trying to figure out how to break the news to you," she said softly.

"And the lawyer you were seeing…"

"Last night I was so shocked, so flustered, that I asked the advice of some friends. They told me I should check with a lawyer before telling you anything."

She wasn't sure how he would respond to that, but the comment brought no immediate response, so she didn't think he was offended by the move.

"I still don't know how the hospital could have made such an error," he said, rubbing at a spot between his eyes.

Cara stood and retrieved a framed photo from the side table. In it, two infant children slept through their first hospital portrait.

"When they were first born, we thought they might be identical twins. They were bald with blue eyes…"

Sensing what she was trying to say, Ross removed his wallet and flipped it open to reveal the pictures of two more infant children.

"They look alike," Cara breathed. "They could be quadruplets if we went by these photographs."

Ross breathed deeply. "So they *could* have been switched at the hospital."

"Let's face it. Mistakes like that rarely happen, but they do happen."

He frowned, his thumb caressing the photograph. "Which leaves us with a dilemma." He looked at Cara, his eyes intent. "What do we do now that we've discovered the error?"

Chapter Five

Cara bit her lip and tried to read Ross's thoughts from the expressions that raced across his face.

What *would* they do now? Had sharing the news with Ross eased the burden? Or had she merely acquired a whole new set of troubles?

But even as the thought came, Cara knew that there would have been no way to avoid the inevitable. Ross Gifford had a right to know the truth, and if she had delayed the news, she only would have made things worse.

When he remained silent, she asked, "What are you going to do now?"

"I don't know."

He stood and began to pace the narrow confines of the room. A deep line slashed between his brows. His strides were quick and powerful, and Cara had the impression of a tiger that had been unexpectedly caged.

"Your girls. What are their names?"

She didn't fault him for not remembering. His mind was probably still stuck on the discovery he'd just made.

"Heidi and Zoe."

"And the one who looks like my wife is..."

She felt something akin to a pang touch her heart. *The one who looks like my wife.* He spoke of his wife as if she were still alive.

"Zoe. Zoe is the redhead."

Tension settled into the muscles of her jaw, even though she told herself that she shouldn't feel threatened by the question. He wasn't making a claim on the child, he was just asking for information.

Wasn't he?

"Your brother and his wife. Did either of them have red hair?"

She shook her head. "We have no redheads in our family that we know of. Zoe's coloring always puzzled us. I guess now we know...or I know."

She bit her lip, reminded again that she was alone in making whatever decisions had to be made. The actions and responses she made from this moment on would determine much of the children's future.

Ross was pacing again. His features had grown

even harder, if that was possible, but Cara couldn't even guess at the emotions he must be feeling.

He must be a hell of a lawyer, she realized. If he was able to keep his thoughts so skillfully hidden, he must terrify his adversaries. She shivered, glad that she would not be facing this man on the witness' stand.

From the corner of her eye Cara noted that the children had returned and were watching Ross from the doorway. Their faces were smeared with chocolate and crumbs, and they had never looked more adorable to her.

"What were they like, your brother and sister?" Ross asked.

Cara flicked a glance from Ross to the children. "They were good people. My brother was sensitive and funny and smart. His wife was petite and clever and talented."

"What happened?" The question was offered without a shred of emotion. Cara had grown so accustomed to people offering their immediate sympathies that she found the question unnerving—especially when coming from someone who had experienced a similar tragedy.

Again her gaze darted to the children, but they had tired of the grown-ups and were moving toward the television. Within moments they were focusing their attention on the television and the antics of Elmo and Big Bird.

"They were killed in a car accident. A drunk driver crossed the median and slammed into them head-on."

Ross winced.

"And your wife?" she breathed, needing to know.

"Cancer. She died soon after the twins were born." He looked at the children again. "How long have you had them?"

"They've been living with me for a year but I became their legal guardian six months ago." She wiped her palms down her dress, hoping that he wouldn't see they were moist.

"You were appointed their legal guardian?"

Her stomach twisted. "Yes. I've already begun formal adoption proceedings."

She wasn't sure if she should have offered the information, but she knew that Ross would find out the details of the arrangement soon enough. It would be better for all concerned if she were honest from the start.

"The children are dealing with the loss?"

"They seem to be. They miss their parents and occasionally ask for them, but the trauma of their deaths seems to be fading. They've even begun to call me Mommy rather than Auntie Cara."

Again she bit her lip to hide the telltale spasm of emotion that gripped her. She still had so many mixed feelings about being called Mommy. She was pleased the twins had accepted her and thrilled that they loved and trusted her as a parent, but she also felt uncomfortable supplanting the role her sister-in-law had played in the twins' lives. She didn't want the twins to forget their parents, even though time had already begun to erase the memories.

Ross paused, his hands resting on his hips. For long moments he stared at the children, then at the carpet.

At that moment Cara would have done anything to read his thoughts. But he continued to wear an inscrutable mask, giving her no clue to the workings of his mind or his heart.

"I've got to go," he said abruptly.

Cara was sure she'd misheard. "What?"

But Ross didn't respond. He was already turning and heading toward the door.

Panicked, Cara jumped to her feet and hurried after him.

"No, you can't just leave. Not yet." Without thinking, she touched his arm, then wished she hadn't. A hot spark ignited at that tiny point of contact and raced through her body, leaving her stunned.

Ross had felt it, too, she knew he had, because

he stared at the spot where her hand touched his sleeve. When he looked up again, his eyes were dark. He had beautiful eyes, rich espresso-brown eyes. If only they weren't so guarded, so...

Bleak.

Her stomach flip-flopped with a fresh bout of nerves.

"You can't just leave," she insisted, forcing herself to concentrate on the twins and their future rather than her own inexplicable yearning to soften the grief that radiated from Ross like an invisible force field. "We've got to talk this out."

Ross pulled away from her, his hand reaching for the doorknob.

"I've got to think about this." When she opened her mouth, he added, "Alone."

Again she reached for his arm. "No. I need to know what you're considering."

Ross sighed. "I don't know what I'm considering. I don't know anything." He glanced at the children. "All I know is that a piece of my wife is sitting on your living room floor watching cartoons, and until a few minutes ago I didn't even know she existed. I'm stunned and...at a loss."

He speared Cara with a glance that chilled her to the bone, then continued, "But my first gut reaction is that she should be with her biological sister. Just as Becca should be with her biological twin. It's a crime to keep them apart.''

Immediately Cara was on her guard. Was Ross trying to tell her that he was contemplating legal action? Was he thinking of claiming Zoe—who with her red hair and blue eyes was obviously his late wife's biological child?

Dear sweet heaven, what had she done? From what Cara had been able to gather, Ross was a powerful man with even more powerful connections. Could he stake a claim on one child? On them both?

Fear flowed through her veins in an icy wave. No. *No!* She couldn't let him take Zoe away. She couldn't let him disrupt her little family. Not after they'd suffered so much already.

Feeling much like a tiger protecting her cubs, Cara wrenched open the door, then placed her body between Ross and the children.

''I think you're right,'' she said coldly. ''You'd better leave.''

Ross jerked as if she'd physically pushed him. ''I beg your pardon?''

He was clearly surprised by her sudden stand, and that fact gave her courage. ''You'd better go. Now.'' She pointed at the two girls seated on the floor. ''Those are my girls. Mine. And don't you dare talk about taking them away from me. I won't allow it, do you hear me?''

''Cara, I—''

''No. I'm not going to listen to you anymore. This is *my* house and these are *my* children and I think the time has come for you to go.''

The muscle in Ross's jaw tensed. ''Fine. But we'll be talking about this again. Soon.''

As soon as he'd cleared the door, Cara slammed it behind him, then twisted the dead bolt. As she whirled to press her back against the panels, she watched the children bickering over ownership of the remote control and felt huge sobs well up from her heart.

What was she going to do if Ross decided to fight her for the children?

Her legs suddenly lost their strength, and she sank to the ground and began to cry.

What am I going to do?

ROSS SOON DISCOVERED that returning to his own home, to his own children, would not help him pull his thoughts together. He went through all the motions—greeting the twins, informing Stibbs of his discovery, even calling his lawyer. But he couldn't have repeated a single statement that any of them had made. The day was a blur, a moment after Cara had opened her door to reveal her children.

As he stared into the darkness of his bedroom late that night, Ross willed himself to relax. But the exercise was futile. Try as he might, he couldn't escape the reoccurring image of those two little girls—girls identical to his own except for the shorter haircuts.

His mind kept telling him that the whole situation was impossible. Hospitals didn't make mistakes. They had security measures to prevent such things from happening. Ross remembered the plastic security bands he and his wife had worn—and the corresponding bracelets attached to the babies' ankles.

But the twins hadn't been born in the delivery room. There had been a delay in banding the babies due to the confusion of the storm and so many expectant mothers arriving at once. A delay that had obviously allowed time for an error to occur.

His stomach clenched, and he felt a sharp stab of pain deep in his gut—the same kind he'd been experiencing more and more often of late. He was probably heading straight for an ulcer. With his caseload, the death of his wife and now this, heaven only knew he'd earned one.

But he didn't want to dwell on that now. He had to concentrate on the twins. Two sets of twins. One set biologically his, and the other...

His jaw hardened. It didn't matter that Brianne wasn't biologically his. She had become his daughter the moment she'd been placed in his arms. He didn't need blood ties. His bond to her was as strong as if his wife had given birth to her—and he wouldn't give her up.

But neither could he ignore the little redhead living under Cara's roof.

He willed himself to relax, taking deep calming breaths. *What would Nancy have thought of these events if she'd lived?*

No. He couldn't think about that now. He couldn't think about his wife or her death or her sweet, sensitive soul. He had to keep his mind on the present. On the twins.

Naturally, there were things that would have to be done. The lawyer in him knew there were tests that would have to be taken in order to confirm the biological identities of the children. He would need to research the legal precedent of such a situation. An investigation of negligence within the hospital would need to be made. Negotiations with Cara concerning the futures of the children would have to be instigated.

His gut twisted again at the mere thought. Only twenty-four hours ago, he'd been toying with the idea of seeing Cara again—on a purely personal level. He'd envisioned asking her to dinner or a night at the ballet.

Ross sighed. If he'd ever thought that something might develop between Cara and him, such ideas were doomed now. She was obviously terrified of the threat he represented in her life.

But as much as he longed to reassure her, he couldn't. The little redhead in Cara's care was so much like his own Becca—and so much like his late wife—that there was no doubt in Ross's mind of her biological origins. How could he turn his back on that discovery?

Yet, therein lay the dilemma.

He groaned when his mind returned to the same arguments he'd made to himself a hundred times already. If he'd been asked to consult on such a case only a day before, he would have claimed it was a travesty of justice to uproot a three-year-old child from the only family she had ever known in order to return her to her biological family. But now that he was faced with that very prospect regarding his own children, the issue was so much more complex. Not only did he have a daughter living under another person's roof, there was Brianne to consider, as well. Just as Zoe was so obviously his, Brianne looked so much like Cara's brother there was no denying her parentage. And like Cara, Ross would fight to the death to keep

Brianne with the family she'd known since birth. The little girl had already suffered so much with Nancy's death, to be given away like a weaned puppy—

He couldn't bear to think about it.

But neither could he bear for either Becca or Brianne to grow up without knowing their biological twins.

So what was he going to do? There had to be a solution to this mess. One that wouldn't tear his family apart. They'd been through so much already.

Think. Think!

But as the night wore on, the enormity of the situation sank into Ross's consciousness, and he reeled from the decisions awaiting them all. There were no simple answers, no easy solutions, merely more heartache for everyone involved.

Rubbing the ache in his stomach, he gave up all pretense of sleep and flipped on the lamp. As the buttery glow flooded the room, he stared at the picture of his late wife that he kept on the bedside table.

The past two and a half years had been a painful journey from grief to acceptance to some semblance of a normal life. He'd been devastated by his wife's illness and subsequent death, but somehow he'd managed to survive. But now, just when he'd dared to think that he might be capable of being attracted to someone other than Nancy, this had happened.

Ross supposed that if he had to choose someone other than Nancy to be the mother to one of his children, someone like Cara would be a definite possibility. Ross wasn't usually a person prone to snap judgments, but from the moment he'd stepped into her home, he'd been struck with the charm of the little bungalow. The air had been redolent with the scent of chocolate chip cookies. There were puzzles and toys stacked in baskets that had been left in easy reach—and those toys he'd seen scattered on the floor had been obviously educational. Her warmth around her children had been so open and obvious. And even though she was new to motherhood, it was clear that she had a knack for making Heidi and Zoe feel happy and secure, despite the recent loss of their parents. Even Ross's children had been smitten with her. They kept asking when the nice lady with the puppets was going to visit again.

If he had to choose a mother for a daughter he'd never known about…

No. He couldn't bear to think of leaving things as they were. He couldn't ignore the fact that Zoe was out there and that two sets of twins deserved to be together. Somehow he and Cara would have

to come to a working solution. Shared custody,
or…

His stomach tightened at the thought, and then
the pain came again when another worry came
swiftly on its heels. He'd spooked Cara tonight by
insisting that the twins deserved a chance to know
one another. Cara had confided in him that the
adoption wasn't finalized yet. If she feared her custody was in jeopardy, she might bolt and take the
twins with her.

He began pacing the bedroom in open agitation.

No. He couldn't let that happen. Somehow he
had to find a way to ensure that she and the twins
remained nearby until things could be worked out.

Unless…

An idea flashed through his brain, one that was
so easy, yet so unnerving that he immediately dismissed it.

No. He wouldn't even consider such a thing. It
was too drastic…too final.

But even as he told himself he was being crazy,
he couldn't help thinking…if he had to choose a
mother for a daughter he'd never known about—a
mother for all of the children?

Ross shook his head. He was out of his mind.
Completely out of his mind. He had known Cara
for less than twenty-four hours and already he was
infusing far too much into their chance meeting.

He didn't even know the woman. So what if she made cookies? A lot of women made cookies. So what if her house was inviting and her children adoring and his own twins curious. That didn't mean that he should be thinking of Cara in terms of…

A wife?

He groaned, raking his hands through his hair. He needed a vacation or some time off.

But the situation that had developed didn't allow for such luxuries. He needed a solution to the problem, and he needed one now.

But marriage?

No. It was out of the question. Absolutely out of the question. He'd been married and he'd loved every minute of it. A man didn't get that kind of luck twice in a lifetime. He and Nancy had been a love match. They'd known each other for years. He was a one-woman man even beyond the grave. Until Cara, he hadn't even been tempted to date again.

Until Cara.

What was it about this woman that she seemed to have a hold over him that went far beyond the dilemma with the children? All totaled, he'd been with her for only a few hours and he was already contemplating…

Marriage?

No. It was preposterous. It was completely un-reasonable. It was...

Such a simple solution that it was almost scary.

No. A person didn't get married just to sort out custody.

Or did they?

Cara would never go for it. She didn't know anything about him.

But she loved her children and would probably do anything to ensure their health and happiness.

That didn't mean she would marry a person like him—a person who was contemplating such a cold, practical marriage of convenience for his own children's sake.

Or would she?

Chapter Six

Cara didn't hear a word from Ross Gifford for two full days. By that time she was pacing the confines of her house. She couldn't eat or sleep. She kept circling the telephone, worried that Ross would never call, then fearing that he would.

The children sensed that something was wrong—which meant that they sought her attention as a way to reassure themselves that she wasn't angry with them. Unfortunately, their methods of seeking attention usually involved getting into trouble. Heidi had tried to flush her shoes down the toilet; Zoe had eaten paint. They'd both colored on the walls with their crayons, left a bag of popsicles to melt in the middle of the kitchen floor and given the neighbor's cat a haircut. Cara had never been so exhausted in her whole life. Emotionally and physically.

Cara's only jaunt out of the house had been to consult with her lawyer, but he'd been unable to offer her any real comfort. Her adoption hadn't been finalized, so her legal position in the twins' lives wasn't as strong as he would like. He would have to make inquiries, research legal precedents, yada, yada, yada. Cara hadn't been able to concentrate on a word after the phrase "Without the adoption being completed, your role as legal guardian isn't as strong as I would like."

Through it all Cara's nerves stretched thinner and thinner. So when she woke up one morning to find three local camera crews and a network anchorman camped out on her front doorstep, the fragile grip on her emotions snapped.

Grasping the phone, she punched in the numbers to Ross's house—making the very call that she had attempted a half dozen times, then aborted.

"Good morning, this is the Gifford residence, Stibbs speaking."

"Put Ross Gifford on the phone. Right this minute!"

She didn't know if it was the frantic edge to her tone or the fact that Stibbs recognized her voice, but a silence was soon followed by "Ross here."

"This is Cara. I want you at my house. *Now.*"

Not giving him a chance to respond, she hung up the phone and quickly moved from window to window, pulling blinds and drawing the curtains closed.

"Mommy, what's wrong?"

Heidi stood in the doorway, rubbing her eyes, her arms wrapped around her favorite stuffed rabbit.

Cara tried to smile reassuringly, but her lips felt stiff. "Nothing's wrong, sweetie. What's got you out of bed so early?"

"There's a man at my window."

It took a moment for the words to sink into her brain. "There's a man at your window?"

Heidi nodded and yawned. "He's takin' pictures."

A white-hot, uncontrollable fury spilled through her veins. It didn't take a rocket scientist to guess why the media was suddenly interested in this house and its occupants. And since Cara hadn't told anyone about the switching of the twins, other than her partners and her lawyer, that left one logical explanation.

Ross. Damn the man.

The emotions that had been simmering for days erupted. Without thinking, she grabbed the broom from its spot in the pantry and marched to the door.

"Heidi, go get your sister and move into the living room. Turn on the television if you want, but stay away from the windows, do you understand?''

Heidi nodded, her finger slipping into her mouth—a habit left over from babyhood and a clear sign that she was worried or upset.

Slamming out of the back door, Cara rushed around the side of the house. Seeing a man in jeans and a dirty sweatshirt priming a camera with an enormous lens at her children's bedroom window, she started swinging.

"Get out, get out, get out!"

She whacked him on the shoulder, then, when he held up a hand to defend himself, she began hitting him on the top of his head.

"Hey, lady! I'm with the *National Expositor* and we'd like to pay you—"

"Out!"

She hit him again and again, slowly driving him toward the front yard. As soon as he was past the myrtle bushes, she brandished the broom like a baseball bat.

"Get out of here. All of you! You have no business here."

"Hey, lady, we've got word that a story is breaking here. Something about switched twins."

Cara was so furious she was shaking. "There's no story. Pack up your gear and clear out!"

"We've got a right to be here. The public has a

right to hear about any mistakes made by the local hospitals.''

Cara could have screamed. Instead she forced herself to say, ''Get off this lawn and off my property or I'll have you arrested for trespassing. You have thirty seconds and then I let the Doberman loose.''

As she whirled back in the direction of the house, she had some satisfaction in seeing the reporters scrambling to get off her lawn.

''Now if I only had a Doberman,'' she grumbled to herself as she stormed back to the house and slammed the door.

For several seconds she stood in the middle of the kitchen, her broom held high and her body trembling with adrenaline. But as the surge of energy began to drain away, she felt her throat growing tight and tears pressing at the backs of her eyes.

How could Ross Gifford have done this to her? She'd been so careful not to tell anyone, knowing instinctively that it was important to keep the whole affair a private matter.

Without even consulting her, he'd made a public spectacle of her children—of her. No doubt, there would be pictures of Heidi and Zoe splashed across the evening paper—as well as one or two of Cara dressed in the oversize T-shirt, baggy boxer-style shorts and ankle socks that she'd worn to bed the previous evening.

Damn him! What had he been thinking when he'd gone to the press with the story? Had Ross already begun maneuvering in an effort to win public sympathy for his plight? After all, Ross Gifford was Zoe's biological father where Cara was only her—

Her what? Her aunt? Could she even lay claim to that title if Ross were to challenge her for custody of the girl?

But wouldn't anyone realize that after all these months she had become so much more to the children and they to her?

She heard the ringing of her front door, then the faint calls of, "Mr. Gifford, Mr. Gifford!"

Marching toward the front door, she decided that the time had come for Ross Gifford to explain everything—including his intentions for the future.

Ross HAD KNOWN there was trouble the moment Cara had called. Her tone had revealed a woman at the breaking point.

Damn. He'd known that he should have called her earlier—and he didn't suppose that his hesitance in contacting her again helped his cause any. But he hadn't wanted to commit himself to any course of action until he'd thought about all of the ramifications. After all, he was considering asking a woman to marry him. A woman he'd only met on two occasions. Granted, he had liked what he'd already seen, but was that any way to choose a mother for his children?

So he'd spent two days trying to talk himself out of the decision. He'd concentrated on business and researching legal precedents regarding children who had been switched at birth.

But he hadn't come up with a way to solve the problem as neatly and painlessly as a quick, simple marriage.

He'd been ready to ask her. Last night, he'd taken a slow shower, shaved and splashed cologne on his cheeks. And then, looking in the mirror, he'd broken into a cold sweat.

No. Marriage wasn't the answer.

But even having made his decision, Ross hadn't slept.

Nor had he called Cara to begin organizing an alternate plan of action.

With the morning traffic, it took nearly fifteen minutes to reach Cara's bungalow. As the minutes passed, Ross tried to come up with a logical reason for his silence the last two days—one that wouldn't involve informing her of his harebrained idea. But it wasn't until he turned onto the block where she lived and he saw the camera crews that he realized just how upset Cara must be.

"Damn," he muttered as he pulled his car into the driveway, deftly maneuvering around the reporters who knocked on his windows and shouted questions through the glass. Curiously, they didn't follow him into the driveway, but stood at the curb just outside the picket fence, jostling for position at the front of the pack.

Ignoring them, Ross slammed the car door, set the alarm in case some ambitious reporter decided to tamper with the Lexus, and strode up the steps of the front stoop. As he jabbed the doorbell, he could feel the cameras being trained on his back.

"Are you responsible for this?"

"Are you suing Cara Wells for custody?"

"How does it feel to discover that you've had your child raised by someone else all these years?"

The door was barely opened before Cara grabbed him by the arm, pulled him inside and then slammed the door shut again. Directing an accusatory finger in the direction of the window, she glared at him, saying, "Why? *Why?*"

Ross held up his hands. As if he didn't have enough to worry about, now Cara thought he was responsible for the press camping out on her doorstep. "I swear, I didn't have anything to do with that mob."

Cara clearly didn't believe him. "Then how did they find out?"

Ross strode to the window, lifting one corner of the shade to peer outside. No one had budged. If anything, the crowd had grown quiet as if they could hear through the walls if they listened intently enough. "My guess is that either someone in the law offices or the hospital leaked the story."

"Law offices?"

Her echo was weak, her eyes wide. Ross shied away from the emotions he saw there—hurt, vulnerability, fear. He had to keep a level head and regard this whole situation as pragmatically as possible.

At that moment a thunder of feet came from the hall, then a loud bump and a high squeal.

Clearly torn, Cara hesitated only a moment, then excused herself. A few moments later Ross could hear her speaking softly to the children, smoothing over the disagreement about a toy, kissing an "owie," offering a glass of milk.

As he heard the voices, Ross felt as if he'd been punched in the stomach. He'd made up his mind, he reminded himself. He'd decided against even mentioning a marriage of convenience to Cara. The whole idea was unreasonable. After all, what right did he have to ask a young, attractive woman to sacrifice her future in that way? They would work something out—shared visitation rights and alternate holidays.

But in that instant when she spoke with her children, Ross's resolve to remain cool and completely detached shattered.

His own children were missing so much. They deserved the influence of a mother who would bake cookies, mediate an argument and heal their imagined ills with a simple kiss. Instead they had a daytime nanny and at night...

A father who adored them but still didn't know quite how to handle a pair of growing daughters. He felt as if he was muddling through the role of father, while Cara, who had been the sole provider for her children for much less time, appeared to be a natural nurturer.

If they were to marry...

No. He couldn't ask any woman to consider such a thing. Ross was honest enough to know that Nancy's death had changed him. He had once been open and filled with a joy for living. But the death of his wife had made his emotions much more guarded. He knew he would never love anyone as he had Nancy. When and if he married again, it would be a relationship based on mutual respect, not love. And if there could be a physical side to such an arrangement, that would simply be an added bonus.

"All better."

Ross immediately focused on the woman standing in the doorway. She looked so vulnerable in her oversize T-shirt and shorts. He doubted that she was even aware of the enticing picture she presented with her sock-clad feet and mussed hair. A nearly perfect set of bright red fingerprints had left a mark on the side of her thigh. Jam, he would bet.

All better. When did a person reach a point in his life when a kiss, a drink of juice and some toast with strawberry jam made everything right again?

Cara tugged self-consciously at the hem of her shirt. "I've sent them to play in their rooms so we can talk alone."

"Your children are very...lively."

Her smile was brief and filled with motherly pride. "If you mean out of control, you're right."

"You seem to have them well in hand."

She grimaced. "We have our days when there's a power struggle, but thankfully the good ones tend to outnumber the bad."

She gestured to a seat, but he shook his head. "I think I'd better say this standing up."

The color leached from her cheeks and he watched as she wiped her palms down the legs of her shorts.

"You've decided to sue for joint custody, haven't you?" she whispered.

Cara had only just met him, yet she knew him so well already. It was almost as if they shared a similar wavelength.

He opened his mouth to agree, then hesitated. Cara was an intelligent, vibrant young woman, who was more than capable of making decisions for herself. So why not go for broke? Why not ask for the unattainable, then work his way back to a more feasible arrangement? Wasn't that the strategy employed for most methods of negotiation?

"I think I've come up with a better solution. It's a little unconventional, but..."

Cara tucked her fingers into her pockets, then nervously removed them again and folded her arms tightly beneath her breasts. If anything, she'd grown even paler, but her hazel eyes glittered mutinously.

"You can't take my children away from me. I won't let you."

The words were barely audible and filled with such pride and protectiveness that Ross's determination was dented slightly. Suddenly he saw himself from Cara's point of view, and it was clear just how much of a bastard Cara thought he was capable of being.

"No. I'm not staking a claim on your children."

"Then what?"

"I think that you would have to admit that the children belong together."

She folded her arms, wrapping them tightly around her as if cold. "Yes. I spoke with one of the university psychologists yesterday morning."

So he hadn't been the only one to investigate their options.

"Studies of twins who have been separated at birth have shown that the absence of a twin can have a negative effect on a child, even if the two children have no knowledge of the other twin's existence. Twins who have been separated tend to feel as if a piece of them is missing."

"Ideally, the children should be allowed to grow up together," Ross agreed slowly.

"I thought you said you wouldn't try to take them away."

He slipped his hands into his pockets. "What I'm suggesting is more of a...merger."

"A merger?" Cara's brow furrowed.

"Of families. Yours and mine."

She blinked. "I don't understand."

"I'm suggesting that we combine the two families into one."

One of her brows rose. "If you think it's a media circus out there now, just imagine what it will look like when we announce that we've decided to cohabit."

Ross slid his hands into his pockets, watching her closely. At the first sign of a flinch he would back off and go back to suggesting shared custody. But right now he had to ask. If he didn't, he would always wonder if he'd done the right thing by pursuing a purely legal avenue to solve their dilemma.

"I'm suggesting a little more than sharing the same house," he stated slowly. "Such a situation would be short-term, and at this point in their lives, I think the children need as much stability as possible. They've already been through more than enough loss for their years."

"Then..."

The time had come. But Ross still hesitated. Once the words were said, they couldn't be taken back.

But even as he considered changing his mind, Ross knew that he had to ask her. He had to follow his instincts, and his gut was telling him to take a chance with Cara Wells.

"I think we should get married."

Ross saw the moment when the idea took root in her mind. Cara's eyes darkened, then widened. Finally she shook her head and moved sharply toward the window. "No. Absolutely not."

"It would solve all of our problems at once. Your children would have a father figure, mine would have a mother. They would have a chance to grow up together as sisters in a stable, healthy environment.''

''Stable? How stable can such a marriage be? I don't even know you.''

He moved slowly toward her. ''I'm not suggesting a love match, Cara. I'm suggesting a marriage of convenience, pure and simple.''

A short laugh escaped her throat. ''You've got to be kidding. This isn't the Middle Ages, and I'm not chattel.''

''I'm not suggesting that you are.'' He let his breath escape in a whoosh. Until now he hadn't realized how much he had hoped that she would agree to his proposition. He thought of all the reasons he could offer to sway her opinion. In an instant his mind, used to the maneuverings of litigation, began formulating his argument and outlining his strategy. But even as he considered presenting his case like a lawyer pleading for his client in a courtroom, he abandoned such a tactic.

This wasn't a trial. It was personal. Very personal.

''Tell me a better way, Cara. Tell me a better way to offer our children the best we can give them.''

Chapter Seven

The moment Ross's words sank into her consciousness, Cara felt the fight drain out of her system.

Tell me a better way to offer our children the best we can give them.

He was right. As much as she balked against the idea of marrying again—especially to a man she didn't even know—that one simple statement put everything into perspective.

Cara would do anything for her two little girls. Anything.

So why couldn't she offer them the chance to live together? To grow up as sisters? To enjoy one another's company, to fight, to laugh, to love?

Because in order to do that, she would have to marry again.

No. I've sworn off marriage. I've sworn off men.

But Ross wasn't suggesting a love match, he

was suggesting a business arrangement. Nobody had said anything about love. She certainly didn't love Ross, she barely knew the man—and she wouldn't expect any emotional declarations from a widower who was still so obviously devoted to his late wife.

"It's nuts," she whispered.

But even as she said the words, Ross parted the blinds to look out at the media crews lining the street. In the space of a few days her quiet life had been turned upside down, and she wasn't naive enough to think that the frenzy of curiosity generated by the media would disappear overnight. Her girls would be forever marked as the "twins who were switched at birth." And she'd seen enough of the media's coverage of similar events to know that the label would haunt them for the rest of their lives.

Unless all of the girls were reunited. Then the fodder for publicity would die after the first meeting.

No. It wouldn't be that simple. A marriage didn't solve all of their problems.

But it would help solve the legalities.

Squeezing her eyes shut, she willed herself to relax, to think. Ever since she'd shut Ross out of her house two days earlier, she had dreaded his decision on how to handle things. His experience as a lawyer had terrified her more than anything else. She hadn't known what to expect—demands for custody of all the children, shared custody, subpoenas, social workers. She'd tortured herself with the possibilities.

Yet, here he was, suggesting a solution that was simple, practical…

And intensely personal.

No. She couldn't do it. Absolutely not. How could she even contemplate living with this man? He was too powerful, too wealthy, too stern and forbidding. She might be physically attracted to him. But *marriage*…

Never. From what she had seen, Ross was too much like her first husband. He was too guarded with his emotions, too structured in his lifestyle. If she were to consider the idea, she would become involved with a man who only wanted to marry her for the sake of convenience—and wasn't that much the same reason Elliot had married her? So that she could be his hostess and trophy wife? Outwardly she'd been the way a perfect wife should be, while inwardly she'd been dying a little more each day.

"I won't live a lie."

"I'm not asking you to."

"You're asking me to pretend to be your wife."

"No. I'm asking you to be my wife. My partner.

I'm not asking you to pretend anything. If anyone asks about the motives surrounding our marriage, we'll be forthright and honest. We married to provide a stable environment for our children.''

She shook her head and jumped to her feet. ''It's nuts. The whole idea is nuts. Arranged marriages went out of fashion along with the horse and buggy.''

''And in the meantime the divorce rate has skyrocketed. Both of us have been married before. We aren't walking into this relationship expecting fairy-tale promises of happily-ever-afters once the vows have been exchanged. Instead we're looking at the whole situation objectively. Although we've only known each other a short while, I think we respect each other. We seem to have a rapport as well as an honest attraction to each other.''

She felt heat seep into her cheeks. Was this Ross's way of letting her know that theirs would not be a platonic relationship?

''You've vowed never to marry, Cara. But you have so much to give. I've only known you a short while, but I've seen the way you are around your girls.'' He hitched a shoulder in the direction of the faint sound of laughter seeping into the silence. ''Don't you think the love you have could extend to my girls, as well?''

When she didn't answer, he moved toward her.

"This marriage might not be a match made in heaven, but it does have all of the necessary ingredients to work. And with that little scrap of paper that legally binds us together, so much would be solved. Gaining guaranteed custody of the children would be little more than a technicality. The media's attention will wane in a few months, rather than years. But best of all, the children could grow up together, with two live-in parents."

Cara bit her lip, her mind skittering from one possibility to the next, seeming to be incapable of settling on any point for long enough to make a decision. Granted, the situation surrounding the twins was untenable, but was marriage the answer?

Ross continued to close the distance between them, his eyes dark and penetrating. And suddenly, even though she knew that a marriage of convenience might be the only viable way to ensure her presence in the children's lives, a part of her still ached at the cold-bloodedness of it all. She might have sworn off marriage, but that didn't mean she'd given up on romance.

But it was just as obvious that romance would have no part in this proposition. Ross had suggested a business arrangement, plain and simple. True, in time, it might grow into a physical relationship, as well. But both she and Ross were emotionally battered and bruised. Neither of them would ever give their hearts so completely again. It simply hurt too much to love and lose—whether it be through death or divorce.

Yet even as she prepared herself for the fact that Ross might never come to love her, she couldn't help wishing that there was some hint of emotion to the proceedings. Did he feel anything for her at all? Even a small measure of empathy for her plight? Would he ever grow fond of her? Or would she have to settle for the passion she'd seen in his eyes when they'd kissed.

No. She wouldn't live a life like that. She couldn't.

Cara opened her mouth, intending to refuse, then hesitated. If she said no, then what were the alternatives? Shared custody? Alternate visits on holidays? It sounded like the aftermath of a divorce, and she'd only known the man for a few days.

So what did she have to lose?

Heaven only knew she had everything to gain.

Stiffening her shoulders, she concentrated on the peal of childish laughter coming from the bedroom. If she agreed to Ross's proposal, there would be two more voices adding to the noise. Two more reasons for her life to be filled with joy.

Closing her eyes, she thought of Ross's children, but what swam immediately into mind was the memory of his house. Instantly she remembered the picture-perfect landscape, the castle-like structure complete with turrets, and the aura of wealth and influence that clung to the estate like a subtle perfume.

Ross Gifford was a powerful man. A lawyer. An influential member of the community, with ties to who knew how many judges and government officials.

And who was she? A nobody. A simple CPA who had no connections outside of those friends and clients she'd met through the Mom Squad.

She had so much to lose.

But if she agreed to Ross's proposal, she would have so much to gain.

And she would do anything for her children.

Anything.

Holding that thought firmly in her mind, Cara met Ross's stare head-on.

"I'll do it."

THEY WERE MARRIED at the Salt Lake City Courthouse. The judge who presided over their vows was a friend of Ross's, and the only guests to attend were Cara's partners and one of Ross's associates.

As she stood before Judge Erickson, Cara wondered for the hundredth time if she'd done the right thing. She'd known Ross for less than a week, yet here she stood in a pale-peach suit, holding a bouquet of roses provided by her friends, promising to love and honor a stranger.

Her limbs trembled as Ross repeated his vows. He was so tall, so forbidding. He was obviously comfortable with their surroundings, because he moved and spoke with a calm sense of confidence, while she quivered in her shoes and wondered how she'd come to this point.

Cara had done a great deal of soul-searching since agreeing to marry Ross—and she'd changed her mind at least a dozen times. But whenever she was tempted to pick up the phone and call off the whole deal, she was reminded again of Ross's power. He had so much going for him. He knew the law inside and out, he had friends in high places, and she had nothing. Nothing but her love for the twins.

In the end she had promised herself that she would give the marriage a try. She would do everything in her power to make it work—for the children's sake. But if there ever came a time when she thought the marriage was more harmful than good, she would leave. She'd lived through one divorce and she could do it again if necessary. She was a survivor, after all. If in the meantime the twins were able to form bonds with one another, the situation would have helped things in the long run. And she would be in a better position as well—looking at shared custody as an ex-wife rather than a ''nobody.''

The judge looked at her, his bristly gray eyebrows lifting, and Cara realized her mind had wandered. Hurriedly she stumbled through her own vows, knowing that the deed was just about done. For better or for worse, she was now Mrs. Ross Alexander Gifford. There would still be legalities to tend to—adoptions of the children so that the law would recognize them as a single family—a process that would take some time. But from the moment she walked out of the judge's chambers, Cara would be married. Again.

She blinked, feeling the sting of tears that she accredited to the stressful situation she'd endured for nearly a week.

You're overwrought, that's all. So much has happened in so little time. Once you've had time to relax, truly relax, you'll be fine.

But even as she reassured herself with such timeworn platitudes, a tiny part of her admitted the truth. Even though she had ''sworn off marriage,'' a corner of her heart had hoped that she might find a love match someday. Secretly she mourned the little girl who had dreamed of a large church wedding with flowers and bridesmaids and an elegant reception.

Even her marriage to Elliot had fallen short of that mark. She'd married Elliot at a busy wedding chapel in Reno between conference meetings. She hadn't even been given the time to change out of her traveling clothes after meeting him at the airport. The ceremony had been rushed and commercially impersonal with tinny, recorded music, a well-used bouquet borrowed for the ceremony and a simple wedding band purchased in the gift shop.

Granted, the ceremony with Ross was more elegant, sophisticated and slightly more personal, but it still lacked something.

Joy. A bride and groom should be eager for their life together to begin.

Instead of being eager, Cara was nervous and dreaded the moments to come. Once they left the judge's chambers, she would be returning to his home to unpack her belongings and settle in. She would spend the rest of the afternoon trying to make herself at home in his cavernous castle. Then she would move the twins' things into one of the bedrooms adjoining the playroom and do her best to make them feel as if they belonged, as well.

Blinking, Cara was suddenly glad that they had decided to wait until after the marriage to introduce the girls to one another. It gave Cara the time she needed to come to terms with her own whirling thoughts. Maybe by then she wouldn't feel as if

her life had suddenly burst into supersonic speed
and she didn't know how to slow it down.

"...now pronounce you Mr. and Mrs. Ross Gifford. You may kiss the bride."

Cara's heart skipped a beat. The ceremony was
over except for the obligatory kiss.

Kiss. The judge wants us to kiss?

If only the judge knew how Cara and Ross had
gone out of their way to avoid touching each other
in the past few days. Instinctively they'd shied
away from the added complications caused by their
attraction to each other and had concentrated solely
on uniting their families.

But now that was done, and the judge presiding
over the services wanted them to kiss.

Her eyes flickered shut as she scrambled to calm
her jangling nerves. She shouldn't be at all surprised by the suggestion. After all, Judge Erickson
couldn't possibly know about the emotionless way
Ross and she had planned this event.

Before Cara quite knew what to do, Ross was
stepping toward her. Bettina had given her a hair
clip of flowers complete with a tiny veil, and Ross
lifted the netting, then stared deeply into her eyes.

Cara shivered at what she saw there. Satisfaction, relief and something else that was deeper and
darker and infinitely more intimate.

Passion.

Possessiveness?

She bit her lip, then released it again when he bent toward her. She had insisted that their marriage remain platonic for a time, but what she saw in Ross's gaze didn't give her confidence that her wish would be granted. Not when her pulse knocked against her throat in response and her body seemed suddenly boneless and warm.

When Ross touched her cheek, the icy grip of her nervousness was unlocked, and she melted into the embrace. When he tipped her head to the side, she willingly complied. And when his lips touched hers...

The world disappeared around them, and she was filled with an instant desire. Her mouth willingly opened, her hands instinctively gripped the lapels of Ross's suit.

Then, just as quickly, he lifted his head and the kiss was over.

Cara stood shaken to the core. Such a simple kiss, only a brief moment of contact. But she thrummed with pleasure and an overwhelming awareness. As their guests gathered around them, she wasn't sure what was being said to her. Cara accepted the words and offers of congratulations with what she hoped was a normal smile, but she was far more conscious of the way Ross slid his arm around her waist and held her tightly against his side. For an instant she felt protected. She could even fool herself into thinking she was loved.

Then, before she had managed to gather her wits, Ross was ushering her into the hot sun outside the courthouse. One by one the other members of the wedding party disappeared, leaving the two of them alone.

Alone.

What was she going to do without the distraction of other people? How was she going to make it through the day without—

Without what? Begging him to forget their platonic arrangement?

Cara inwardly chided herself for being so weak. Perhaps she'd made a mistake by refusing to date after her divorce. If she'd had more of a social life, maybe she wouldn't be so needy. So hungry for—

"Are you hungry?"

Cara started, sure that Ross had read her mind. But when he met his gaze, she realized that his question didn't hold the sensual overtones of her own musings.

Hungry.

Food.

He was thinking of food.

Cara blinked, wondering how Ross could be thinking of something so commonplace as eating at a time like this. But as he ushered her toward his car and released her to unlock her door, her awareness of everyday things returned bit by bit and she realized that she was starving. She hadn't done much more than nibble at food since this whole ordeal had begun days before.

"I could eat," she said as she slid into the supple leather interior of Ross's car.

Even his car was elegant and powerful, gleaming with a fresh cleaning, while hers was in sad need of a vacuuming to get the Cheerios and crumbs off the floor.

Ross slid behind the driver's wheel, and the engine thrummed to life with a muted purr that spoke eloquently of its expensive price tag.

"Where would you like to go?" Ross asked as he backed out.

"You decide."

His lips twitched in the barest impression of a smile. "Now I know we're married."

Cara frowned. "What do you mean?"

"Some of my most frustrating moments as a child came from sitting in the back seat of a car listening to my mother and father exchange such lines as, 'Where do you want to go?' 'You decide.' 'No, you decide.' In the meantime, my father would drive aimlessly around town, passing a dozen different venues until everyone was hungry, frustrated and on edge. Then we would end up at a restaurant where none of us really wanted to eat because we'd already wasted so much time.''

Cara smiled as images of similar car rides flooded her memories. ''Your mother and father are still alive?''

''Mother is. Father passed away from heart trouble when I was in my teens.''

But Ross hadn't invited his mother to the wedding.

''Tell you what,'' Ross said as he turned into the late-evening traffic of downtown Salt Lake. ''I'll drive around aimlessly, and you let me know when something looks good.''

''Pizza.''

''I beg your pardon?''

''I'm in the mood for pizza. And unlike your mother, I'm more than happy to state my wishes before we both get carsick.''

Ross's gaze flicked over her silk suit. ''We'd better change first.''

Within minutes he had reversed the direction of the car and was steadily climbing the eastern bench. With each block they passed, Cara's nervousness increased. Events had happened so quickly. Since they had decided it would be better to live in Ross's larger home, she'd been forced to pack up belongings and list her own house as a rental in a matter of days. In that time she hadn't had a spare minute to discuss living arrangements once inside Ross's castle. She'd been clear about wanting a platonic marriage, but would Ross insist on sharing a bedroom?

She took a quick, calming breath to quell her sudden panic. Why had she allowed things to move so quickly? Why hadn't she demanded that they slow down the preparations to a saner pace?

But as they neared the security gates of Ross's home and saw the mob of news vans and reporters waiting there, she remembered the intrusion of the media in their lives. She and Ross had wanted their marriage to be a fait accompli before reporters got wind of it.

Without even pausing, Ross hit a remote control button and slid into the driveway. Cara expected the reporters to run for the house, but within seconds a pair of security guards—complete with *real* Doberman pinschers—kept the media from swarming inside.

"Nice dogs," she murmured, remembering her own threat to sic an imaginary dog on the reporters who'd come to her house.

"What?"

"Nothing."

Ross touched another button and one of the garage doors rose.

"Are your girls with Stibbs?" Cara asked, still

not used to the fact that she was about to live in a house with a genuine British butler.

"No. Stibbs categorically refuses to tend children. It's one of his little quirks. The girls are staying the night with their nanny, Mrs. Graves." He killed the engine, then regarded her with dark eyes. "I thought it would be a good idea for us to settle in without the children underfoot. Even Stibbs has taken a couple of days off."

So they were alone. Completely alone. Or were they? Ross had once mentioned something about a housekeeper.

"Your housekeeper is here, though, isn't she?"

"No. The daytime cleaning staff has gone for the day. As for the others... I gave everyone but the dozen or so men on the security team the night off."

Team? He had a security *team?*

Ross opened his door, and Cara slid out of the car before he had time to round the car and help her.

The time had come for her to begin her new life as Ross's wife.

Chapter Eight

Wordlessly Ross motioned for her to precede him into the house.

Cara made her way through the mudroom to the kitchen, relying on her memory of her first night in Ross's home.

Has it really only been a week?

Unsure how to proceed once she was inside, Cara paused near the gleaming table and bit her lip, nervously wondering what to do next.

Ross, on the other hand, seemed to have no such qualms. He dropped his keys in a silver bowl on the counter, then leafed through a pile of waiting mail.

Cara waited in silence, wondering if it would be presumptuous of her to begin unpacking her things.

But then, she didn't know where she would be staying. Or if she'd be sleeping alone.

"You'll have to tell me how you want to work with the nanny in the coming months."

Finally, a subject on which she felt comfortable offering her views.

"I don't want a nanny at all," she stated firmly.

Ross paused in the midst of reading a letter, peering at her from beneath a creased brow. "I'm afraid I'll have to insist that you keep her with you at least part-time."

Cara bristled. "Why? I thought you liked the way I handle my own children. I thought that was one of the reasons for this marriage."

"It is. But you've also just inherited another set of children—making it much like having three-year-old quadruplets running around the house. I asked you to be my wife, not my slave. I know from my own experience that the twins can be a handful. It's going to be even more complicated with four of them."

"But you've already got a butler and a house-keeper. It's not as if I'd be running the household single-handedly."

"No, but you also need some time to pursue your own interests, as well as your work with the Mom Squad—or am I wrong in thinking you wanted to continue working?"

"Of course I do."

"Then the nanny stays." He dropped the mail

on the counter and began working at the knot of his tie. "I've also set up a checking account—"

"No. I won't take money from you."

He sighed. "You didn't let me finish."

Cara opened her mouth to reiterate her refusal. She wouldn't take money from him. It would be too much like being a...a kept woman.

A nervous laugh nearly burst from her lips. A "kept" woman? Did anyone even use such a term anymore?

But before she could form a scathing reply, Ross continued.

"I've arranged a checking account with enough money in it each month to take care of the bills and household expenses. I'd appreciate it if you would take over the responsibilities of seeing they get paid. After all, you're a qualified CPA with more than enough experience handling the Mom Squad's finances."

Some of her anger drained away when she realized that he meant to include her in family matters. Inexplicably his suggestion touched her more that he would ever know. Her first husband hadn't trusted her with such a responsibility. She hadn't even known her husband's true income until divorce proceedings had begun.

"You'll need to give me an itemized budget," Cara said.

He shook his head. "This isn't a business, it's a family. If you need more money, you can go to our bank and arrange for the automatic deposit to be increased. If you have money left over, then you can keep it, spend it, or save it—whatever you think best."

Cara wanted to object, but he was being so reasonable, she knew that any arguments she might offer would simply sound childish.

"Is that system agreeable to you?"

"Yes, of course." But her voice was tight.

"I'll also give you the numbers of our other accounts and investments." He dropped the mail on the counter. "I've got life insurance, but we'll need to arrange coverage for you, as well. In any event, I want it clear from the beginning that what I have is yours."

Ross ripped his tie loose and unbuttoned his shirt, revealing a large vee of healthy, tanned flesh. Cara's gaze fixed there. The knot of need inside her tightened.

When she looked up, it was to find Ross watching her closely.

"Come with me," he said, his voice low and silky. "I'll show you where you'll be staying."

Ross led Cara up the ornately carved staircase. Once again she was reminded of that first night she had come to Ross's house. That night she had been awed by her surroundings and completely unaware of the rush of events that would take her by storm the minute Ross opened the nursery door.

This time Cara gazed around her with new eyes, knowing that Ross's castle was to be her home, as well.

Home? She shivered. She didn't know if she could ever feel comfortable in a house that was so large, so steeped in luxury, so...stark and cold.

Cara had always been a person who liked to "nest." She liked soft colors, overstuffed furniture, fluffy rugs, fresh flowers. In the past she had always strived for a sense of coziness in her surroundings. She'd felt it was important that a person feel as if she could take off her shoes and relax the moment she'd crossed the threshold.

Something would have to be done to Ross's home, that much was clear to her. If she was going to live here, she had to make at least one room an oasis of beauty so she could feel at ease. But she didn't know if she dared do anything so mundane as add color, pattern and texture to a room in Ross's house. Ross had probably spent a fortune in decorating fees to obtain its current look. After all, the castle was a showplace—the kind of home where one entertained.

Or courted royalty. In truth, she would have been less surprised to see Robin Hood and Maid

Marian suddenly appear, than someone padding down the hall in stocking feet.

"I hope this meets with your approval."

Ross stopped at a set of double doors opposite the nursery, and her heart thumped in her chest.

"I thought you might want to be close to the children—especially while your own twins are settling in."

"Y-yes. That would be nice."

Her fingers unconsciously pleated the ribbon of the bouquet she still held. Was she about to discover that Ross also shared the same room? After all, they'd just promised to spend a lifetime together. It wouldn't be too much to ask that they share the same bedroom, even platonically.

"I'll leave you here to change. In the meantime I'll get out of my own suit and meet you downstairs."

"Sure." The word was a bare puff of sound. To her infinite relief she watched Ross move away and disappear into a room at the end of the corridor.

So he didn't expect her to share a bed with him.

Taking a deep, fortifying breath, Cara opened the door to the bedroom, then stared. The suite was huge. Huge and ornate and...

"Positively medieval," she murmured, stepping inside, closing the door again and resting her back against the carved panels.

Stark-white walls stretched up and up to a vaulted ceiling edged in ornately carved wood. A four-poster bed complete with a richly embroidered canopy and coverlet had been positioned against one wall, while at the other was a small sitting room. Directly opposite the door was a huge bay window complete with multicolored mullioned panes.

Kicking her shoes off, Cara set the bouquet on a mahogany table and shrugged out of her jacket. An investigation of the other two doors revealed a walk-in closet larger than her previous bedroom and a bathroom complete with a Roman-orgy-size tub, a separate shower and a full dressing area.

"Welcome to the lives of the rich and shameless," she whispered, then paused when she caught sight of her own reflection in the mirror.

"What have you done, Cara m'girl?" she asked softly, repeating the often used phrase her older brother would ask whenever he sensed she'd been up to no good.

But on the heels of that thought came a fierce certainty that she'd done the right thing. She couldn't have competed against a man like this. Not in a million years. She had only to look around her at this house to realize that Ross Gifford had all the necessary tools to get what he wanted. If he'd decided to take Zoe away, a simple CPA wouldn't have been able to stop him.

Her chin tilted defiantly. Which meant that she'd made her decision and she would stick by it. One way or another, she would find a way to make the best of this situation. She might not feel comfortable in his house—or even his life—for the time being. But she could change that. It wasn't as if she were a total stranger to the better things life could offer. She'd rubbed shoulders with the wealthy during her brief marriage to Elliot.

But she was soon beginning to realize that Elliot's wealth was nothing compared to Ross's. She would have to be on her best behavior with Ross's friends and associates.

The moment the thought popped into her head, she grew still. No. She'd played that game with Elliot—trying to mold herself into the woman she thought he wanted so that he would be happy. In doing so, she'd lost more and more of her own identity and self-worth.

Ross Gifford had known what she was before he married her—a simple person with simple tastes. She would be herself around him, damn it. And if he didn't like it, then he could…he could…

Find someone else? Like Elliot had done?

Groaning, she marched into the closet, intent on finding her things. She refused to think any more about the marriage or her role as Ross's wife. If she wanted to keep her sanity, she would need to concentrate on the here and now and not the what-ifs of the future.

Cara quickly found that all of her belongings had been neatly hung on the closet rods or placed in the drawers underneath. Everything had been sorted according to function, style and color with such precision that Cara wondered who was responsible. Was it Stibbs who had been so attentive or the unknown housekeeper and her staff?

Sighing, she grabbed a pair of jeans and a T-shirt, noting to her dismay that both of them had been religiously pressed. In her opinion there was something sad about comfort clothes that had been ironed.

A few minutes later she emerged from her room, her clothes changed, her feet encased in a pair of sneakers and her face washed and sporting only a bare minimum of makeup. If a stand was going to be made regarding her personal preferences, she might as well begin now.

Hearing Ross's voice coming from the front of the house, she jogged down the stairs, her fingers lightly tracing the carved banister. Then she followed Ross's low tones until she reached what looked like a sunroom. Except for the nursery, it was the most casual room she'd seen yet in Ross's

house. A large, round, wrought-iron table was sur-
rounded by potted plants and trellises covered with
clematis. A whole series of floor-to-ceiling French
doors opened onto a brick terrace.

Seeing her, Ross terminated his call. He had
changed from his charcoal-colored suit, but still
wore a pair of tailored trousers and a dark polo
shirt. He looked ready for a round of golf at an
expensive country club.

"Do you play golf?" she asked suddenly.

"Yes, why?"

"Just wondering." Sliding her fingers into her
hip pockets, she turned to stare at the room around
her. Once again, except for the plants, the room
was decorated in a stark grayish-white. "I never
cared for the game, personally," she said, her
words nearly a dare.

"Why is that?"

"I couldn't see the sense in paying money to
chase a little ball around with a stick."

Ross's lips twitched, but not enough to actually
become a smile. "There are some who would say
that the fun of the game comes from just such a
challenge."

"I suppose."

"The pizza should be here any minute."

Cara stiffened. "I thought we were going out."

"Rush hour traffic will be reaching its height

about now, so I figured we might as well have our food delivered and save ourselves some time.''

"Sure.'' Her voice was casual, but inside she was a mass of jangling nerves again. She'd been counting on the noise and bustle of a pizza parlor to cover the awkward silences. Instead she and Ross would be eating alone.

Belatedly Cara realized that Ross hadn't even asked her what kind of toppings she wanted on her pizza. With her luck, he'd probably ordered from a gourmet restaurant and she was about to be fed an exotic concoction of goat cheese and roasted pine nuts.

She was going to have to teach this man to relax.

No. It wasn't her place to change Ross any more than she wanted to him to change her. But she wished there could be a way to help erase the grief from deep in his eyes.

Silence fell around them, and Cara scrambled for something to say to fill the void. Heaven only knew that her own thoughts were far too dangerous for her to dwell on them.

"You've made arrangements for the twins to meet each other tomorrow?''

Ross nodded. "Polly will bring Heidi and Zoe to meet us at the park, then Mrs. Graves will arrive a few minutes later with Becca and Brianne.''

Cara hadn't been surprised when Ross had

checked with a renowned child psychologist to decide how best to reunite the children. They had been told to choose a "neutral" location where the twins could explore one another much as they would any other curiosity.

"How do you think they'll react?"

Cara's fingers worried the bottom of her shirt, and Ross moved forward to take her hand. "They'll be fine. The hard part is over."

Over? Why did Cara think that the challenges had only now begun?

Ross laced his fingers through hers. "You worry too much."

"I can't help it. I keep thinking that we should have taken things more slowly."

"To what end?"

"Maybe we should have let them get used to the idea of us marrying."

"We both agreed that it would be better to handle all of the changes at once and then settle them into a normal, reassuring routine."

"I know, but—"

Ross laid a finger over her mouth. "It's done. Don't worry so much about what could have happened, what should have happened. Life doesn't work that way."

She shivered when he bent toward her, his eyes darkening.

"Life rarely offers us any guarantees, only surprises," Ross whispered against her lips.

Then he was kissing her, his lips warm and intent, his body hard and warm. Cara moaned as the passion flared between them in the space of a heartbeat.

At least we have this, she thought. Their relationship might be unconventional, but they had the building blocks to make something more of it—mutual respect, a love for their children. And this…

Without even thinking, she wrapped her arms around his shoulders. She rose on tiptoe, allowing him to kiss her again and again and again.

They might not have love.

But they did have this.

She held on to him more tightly, drawing from his strength. Would passion be enough? Could a marriage based on convenience really last?

"Yo! Ross!"

The shout caused them to break apart like guilty teenagers. Ross was the first to react. Raking his fingers through his hair, he called, "In here, Tony."

But when he looked at Cara, it was as if he was saying, "Later."

Later?

For what?

Chapter Nine

To Cara's infinite surprise, the pizza hadn't been delivered to their door by a teenage delivery boy but by a large Italian with a booming laugh.

"Paesano!"

"Tony, this is my wife, Cara. Cara, this is Tony Palermo, my daughters' godfather."

"Wife!" The burly man's surprise couldn't have been clearer. "Why didn't you tell me you were getting married?"

Cara was wondering the same thing. If this was the children's godfather, why hadn't he been invited to their wedding?

"We wanted to keep things simple and quiet, so we eloped this afternoon."

Tony's laughter boomed through the small room. "That explains why we weren't invited." He grinned at Cara. "My Graziella is a wonderful woman and a heavenly cook, but she's a born gossip. If you give her a piece of news, she'll have it spread all over town in a heartbeat.''

Tony set the insulated carriers down on the table and enfolded Cara in a quick hug.

"Congratulations to both of you!" As Tony released Cara, he pointed a finger in Ross's direction. "It looks like you finally took my advice and found a woman to brighten up the place."

Ross grimaced good-naturedly and began unloading the insulated bags.

"First thing you do, Cara, is slap a coat of paint on these walls."

Ahh, a soul mate. Evidently Cara wasn't the only one who found Ross's decorating austere.

"I take it you're a frequent visitor."

Laughing, Tony slapped Ross on the back. "She hasn't caught on to you yet, has she?" He winked at Cara. "He and the twins give me a call at least three or four times a week. They don't much like the housekeeper's cooking, if the truth is known."

"Now, Tony," Ross protested.

Tony winked at Cara. "I come often enough to have my own key card to the security gate—and if that isn't a telling detail, I don't know what is. Even the housekeeper doesn't have one of those."

"Tony..."

Tony interrupted whatever Ross had been about

to say with another booming laugh. Then he began flipping box lids open to reveal the food he'd brought with him. The first box held a large pizza, smothered—not with goat cheese and pine nuts as she'd feared—but pepperoni, ham and sausage. A smaller container held a loaf of garlic bread, and yet another sack had a plastic bowl with a green salad tossed in vinaigrette.

As Cara settled into her seat, it was Tony who disappeared into the kitchen to return with plates, utensils and glasses. Ross soon followed with bottles of soft drinks, and all three of them sat around the table.

"So you and Ross are old friends?" Cara asked, her mood improving by the minute as the heavenly aromas promised her a real treat.

"He saved my life."

"Hardly."

Tony waved aside Ross's protest.

"He did. Honest."

"I merely handled your sister's divorce."

"And if you hadn't, I would have killed the bastard she'd married, so there you are. I would have been given a life sentence at the very least."

Tony grinned, watching as Cara took her first bite of pizza. The expression on her face must have been enough to convince him that she had never tasted anything better, because he continued.

"Since I'm the children's godfather, I drop by on a regular basis to make sure they're eating properly. Those little girls are the highlight of my day. But then, you probably know all about their antics, don't you, Cara?"

She paused while scooping a forkful of salad toward her mouth. "I've only met Ross's children once."

Tony's brows rose and some of his humor vanished. "Really? I would have thought—" He looked at Ross for an explanation.

"We were married rather suddenly. We haven't known each other for very long."

"How sudden was this courtship?"

"Less than a week."

Tony wiped his mouth with a napkin and leaned back in his chair, his eyes wide and his mouth parted in astonishment. His gaze bounced from Ross to Cara, then back to his friend, and some of the joy disappeared beneath open curiosity.

"So what's the scoop?"

Ross looked at Cara before continuing, but she didn't object to having Tony know the truth. It would be best that those closest to them know everything from the beginning.

"Cara has a set of twins, as well."

Ross reached into his pocket to retrieve his wallet, removing the picture of his own twins and one of Cara's. Then he set the two photographs in front of Tony.

"We thought a marriage between us might be the best solution."

Tony was speechless for several long minutes. Finally he lifted the pictures, squinting at one and then the other.

"I don't understand," he finally said.

"Neither do we. As near as we can tell the twins were switched sometime in the hospital."

"It's amazing." Tony looked up again. "You're not just pulling my leg, are you?"

Ross shook his head.

"So you decided to marry to take care of things?"

"It seemed the easiest way."

Tony took a deep breath and chuckled again. "Simpler, maybe, but I wouldn't say easy. No marriage is easy. It takes work. It always takes work."

He handed the pictures back to Ross, then jerked his thumb in the direction of the window. "Am I to assume that it's *your* marriage that's responsible for that mob at the gate?"

Ross shook his head. "Somehow they got word of the twins, but not our marriage. Not yet, anyhow."

Tony rolled his eyes. "And here I was thinking

you must have got hired to handle another messy divorce.''

Cara's eyes widened at the comment. No wonder Ross hadn't come unglued at the sight of the reporters still swarming around his front gates. Judging by Tony's words, the situation wasn't entirely new to Ross.

Which meant she had just inherited a similar relationship with the media, whether she liked it or not.

The edge of her hunger disappeared as Cara realized there was still so much she didn't know about her husband.

How many more surprises waited in the wings?

''Yep,'' Tony said, interrupting her thoughts, ''a marriage takes work.'' Tony murmured again, more to himself than to Cara and Ross, ''It always takes work.''

A MARRIAGE TAKES WORK. It always takes work.

The words came back to haunt Cara when Tony eventually gathered the empty containers, offered Cara a huge bear hug, then drove away into the night amid the burps and groans of his ancient delivery van.

Cara sighed as she watched Tony disappear. The quiet evening gathered around her and she willed herself to stay relaxed. After all, the night sky was filled with stars and the cool breeze brought with it the heady perfume of flowers from the garden.

But try as she might, Cara couldn't help feeling as if she'd been plunked down in the middle of Oz. She didn't belong here. She wasn't a woman who was comfortable with any display of ostentation. She'd tried that life and it hadn't worked. What made her think that she would be any better at it now?

"It's a beautiful night."

Ross's low comment slid over her like a silken caress.

"Yes. Yes, it's lovely."

It was their wedding night and the two of them had been left alone at this fairy-tale castle as if they were in need of a proper honeymoon.

The thought made her shiver, but not from the cool breeze. There had been no pretence offered with their marriage of convenience. So why had everyone insisted that they spend the evening alone like passionate newlyweds? She would have preferred having the children nearby. Noisy, boisterous, loving children. Maybe then it wouldn't have seemed so...lonely.

Suddenly, there was a sparkle of light deep in the trees, then another.

"What was that?" Cara asked, realizing that it

had come from a point near the front security gates.

"A flash. Some fool is trying to take flash pictures from hundreds of yards away."

Which meant there were at least a dozen other journalists who weren't so foolish, filming them even now with telephoto lenses or night vision.

She wrapped her arms around her and shivered despite the warmth of the evening. "Surely they know that we're married now. Isn't their story over?"

"The story won't be over until we settle into a dull predictable routine. I'd guess they're waiting around to see if the marriage appears to be a happy one or to document any unpleasantness that might occur after such a hasty match. Then there's the matter of the children. They're hoping to get shots of the reunion as well as their everyday play."

The mere thought of all those prying eyes made Cara feel suddenly weary. "I wish they would go away."

"They will. Eventually. Once they've discovered that they are wasting their time peering at a normal, mundane family."

Normal family. Right. A normal family who lived in a castle complete with married strangers and two sets of identical twins who were switched at birth.

"I've been through media storms before," Ross continued on. "It's best to ignore the reporters, let them get their pictures and their facts. We might even issue a press release or conduct a short interview with one of the more trusted national affiliates. When that's through, our lives will be our own."

So why didn't Cara believe him? Why didn't she think that the press would give up so quickly? Was it because she had her own doubts about the solidity of their marriage of convenience?

Stop it. You've only been Ross's wife for a few hours. You can't start doubting yet.

Suddenly, Cara was filled with an anger at the reporters who waited like vultures on the other side of the security wall. She was angry at their willingness to provide the world with sensational news—news that came at Cara's expense, and her children's.

"Why don't we give them something to report about," she said lowly, turning to Ross.

"What?"

It was clear his mind had already moved on to other things, but Cara didn't let that dissuade her. Her hands slid up his chest and hooked around his neck, pulling him toward her.

"They want pictures, so let's give them pictures." Then she was pressing her lips to Ross's.

Ross's surprise lasted only a minute. Then his own arms slid around her waist and drew her against him, tightly, completely—so much so that she felt as if they were two halves to a whole.

But if they had thought to offer a performance for the media, their own desire soon swamped anything but the need to touch, to caress, to kiss. With a moan, Ross's mouth opened, and their kisses grew immediately hungry and wild as they strained against one another.

Ross's arms slid low beneath her hips, lifting her against him. Gasping for breath, she arched her head back, but Ross wasn't dissuaded. Instead, he began to string kisses down the sensitive column of her neck to the hollow at the base of her throat.

She gasped when a molten heat pooled in her belly. No man had ever inspired such an instantaneous passion in her. Ross had only to touch her and she was on fire. It wasn't fair. No man should have such power over her. She should have the will to resist him.

But you don't want to resist, her conscience whispered—and it was true. In Ross's embrace, she felt like a whole woman, one who was desirable, powerful, and needed.

Needed. Elliot had never made her feel needed. She'd been a living prop to him, not a wife. As she bent to kiss Ross again, she realized that despite their unconventional marriage, she felt more of a part of this man's life than she ever had with Elliot.

In one smooth movement, Ross bent and slid his arms beneath Cara's knees. Then he was carrying her into the house and shutting the door with his shoulder.

A part of her knew that her defenses were weakening. But she couldn't seem to remember why she should resist him. Not when her body was on fire and her pulse raced. She supposed that she should have more pride, that she should stick up for herself and her insistence on a platonic relationship. But at this point, she didn't care. She merely wanted the madness to continue.

Ross shifted her in his arms, setting her feet on the ground. With his hands on either side of her, he kissed her deeply, intimately, his body straining against hers. Then, just as suddenly, he broke away.

It took several moments for Cara to realize that it wasn't Ross who held her upright, but the thick carved panels of the door. Rather than being held in Ross's embrace, she was alone. He stood several yards away from her, his back turned in her direction.

''That should give them something to splash on

their front covers,'' he muttered breathing hard, his voice hoarse.

Cara bit her lip, infinitely hurt. Was that all the embrace had been to him? A means to fight back at the media?

No. There had to be more to it than that.

But then again, why should she think that Ross had felt anything more than a burst of passion? After all, it had been her idea that they kiss for the media, not his. For all she knew, he hadn't wanted to kiss her at all. Could she really blame him now if he'd had enough?

Yes. Because I want him to feel more. I want him to feel as completely swept away as I was.

Shame filled her soul when Cara acknowledged to herself that if Ross had continued to carry her up the carved staircase to one of the bedrooms above, she wouldn't have offered an argument. She would have willingly made love to him, thereby breaking her own vow to keep their relationship purely a matter of convenience.

Was she really that desperate? Was she really that hungry for companionship that she would jump into bed with the first man who made such overtures?

But with a sinking heart, she was forced to admit that not just any man would do. In the space of little more than a week, she had grown to care for

Ross Gifford. So much so that even now she shied away from labeling the depth of her need.

"I'm going to my room now," she stated softly.

Then, before she lost what shreds of pride she still gripped and begged him to come with her, she ran upstairs and shut herself inside her bedroom.

Alone.

Ross WAITED UNTIL he'd heard her door snap closed before allowing the breath he'd been holding to ease from his lungs.

She only had to touch him and he was on fire.

Ross raked his fingers through his hair and slowly made his way to the kitchen. Once there, he took a cold container of bottled water from the inner doorway and placed it against his forehead.

But even the icy condensation against his skin couldn't make him forget the velvety texture of Cara's flesh against his, the silken heat of her mouth.

Dear sweet heaven, was he so out of control of his own urges that he would force himself on a woman who had insisted on a platonic relationship? Had he so quickly forgotten that she wouldn't have touched him at all if it hadn't been for the media watching them from afar? Cara had merely wanted to establish their "compatibility"

for the reporters and he had held on to her as if
they were…

Married?

Air. He needed some air.

Slamming the bottle down on the counter, Ross
made his way onto the rear deck. But even the cool
kiss of the evening breeze couldn't erase the scent
of Cara's perfume from his mind, the delicious
touch of her fingers at his back.

What was it about this woman? What part of her
personality had the ability to completely swamp his
common sense? Time and time again, he'd reiter-
ated to himself that theirs was to be a business-like
arrangement. She would help him with the children
and the household responsibilities, and he would…

He would what? What was he contributing to
the bargain? What benefits was Cara gaining from
the relationship? The security of her role as the
children's mother, surely, but what more was he
willing to offer her?

Willing? Why had he used that particular word?

Shame gripped at his stomach.

Because he didn't know how much he could invest in the arrangement. Cara was more than welcome to his money, his home and every other
financial enticement he could offer—but she'd already made it clear that she wasn't overly inter-

ested in such things. So that left Ross with what
he was willing to give her emotionally.

Squeezing his eyes shut, he feared that he
couldn't offer her enough. Friendship, yes. A certain fondness, yes. Passion, definitely. But anything more than that…

No.

As much as he might want it to be otherwise,
he didn't have anything more than that left to give.

Chapter Ten

After their "intimate wedding night," Cara couldn't wait to retrieve the children. She wanted to hug Heidi and Zoe close and to revel in the sound of their laughter. She wanted to reassure herself that they had enjoyed their evening with Polly. Then she wanted to get to know Becca and Brianne.

Cara took a deep breath, realizing that only a few months ago she had been a single woman intent on the growing demands of the Mom Squad. She'd allowed little else to occupy her time or her thoughts. And now…

Now she was Ross Gifford's wife and the mother of four.

How did it all happen so quickly?

Shaking her head, Cara refused to think about her sudden marriage. She'd already spent a sleepless night worrying and fretting about the whole affair. It was time she shifted her attention to the children. She'd married to provide a better life for all of the girls, and it was time she concentrated solely on them.

But even after reminding herself of that fact, Cara had a hard time convincing herself her motives were entirely selfless. Where only the day before she had been looking forward to the moment when the two sets of twins were reunited, in order to see how the girls would react, now Cara longed to have them nearby to help break the tension that was growing between Ross and her.

Nevertheless, as she handed Ross the keys to the Mom Squad van and slid into the passenger seat, she couldn't help feeling a quiver of unease.

She had no idea what was going to happen in the next few hours. Although she had tried to prepare Heidi and Zoe for this moment by telling them that Ross had a pair of twins ''just like them'' and had shown them pictures of Becca and Brianne, she didn't think they'd quite understood. Instead they'd pointed to the pictures time and time again claiming the images as their own.

''This is going to be so confusing for them,'' Cara whispered, raking her fingers through her hair. Then she paused when she caught Ross looking at her. In that instant she thought she saw a hot glow of awareness ignite in his dark eyes. But before she could say anything, he had shifted his gaze and she was left to wonder if the desire she'd seen had merely been a reflection of her own.

"Both Polly and Mrs. Graves have been talking to them about the meeting ahead."

"I know, but it might have been better if..."

"If you were the one to do it?"

"Well...yes."

"You're not the only one having such doubts, Cara. But sometimes it's better to get the truth from a source other than our parents."

She grimaced. "I was hoping the girls would reach puberty before they stopped believing what I tell them. It seems that day will come much sooner than I'd expected."

"Children are born cynical these days."

Cara had to bite her tongue to keep from retorting, "Not mine."

Ross expertly maneuvered the Lexus out of the garage. "I suppose I'll be buying a minivan," he said.

"Oh, really? Why?"

He cast her a quick glance "We won't all fit in the sedan."

Too late, Cara realized that they were now a family of six—*six!* So why did she still think of herself as the mother of two? Why couldn't she seem to make her brain come to terms with the fact that she had married this man for better or worse and accepted the responsibility of becoming the mother to his children?

At least until he tired of her like Elliot had done.

Resolutely she pushed that thought aside. Ross wasn't Elliot. Just because her former husband had been unfaithful didn't mean that Ross was likely to do the same.

So why wasn't she totally convinced? Why couldn't she come to terms with the fact that she had committed to making this relationship work?

Probably because it didn't feel like a relationship. It didn't even seem real. Only a few days had passed, and her world had been shaken to its very core. She was only now beginning to come to terms with the fact that she had gone to extreme lengths to protect her position in her children's lives.

And she'd become an instant mother to another set of twins in the process.

What have I done?

"Smile and wave."

"What?"

She'd been so deep in her thoughts, she barely heard Ross's comment.

"Smile and wave. We're about to reach the gates and our gauntlet of media personnel."

She'd forgotten about them—although, how she'd managed to forget she wasn't sure.

"Pretend you're the queen," Ross advised, already pasting a wide smile on his face.

Even though Cara knew his smile was false, the effect on Ross's features was devastating. For the first time since she'd known him, his features lost their somber cast, and the planes and angles softened.

So this was what he must have looked like before Nancy died.

And he could look this way again if he abandoned his grief.

Cara didn't know why, but the thought brought a measure of peace to her battered spirit, and she felt suddenly lighthearted.

"I'll do one better than the queen," she said as they came to the last bend before the gatehouse.

Ross had already pushed the automatic opener. With the security guards holding the reporters back, it was evident that he intended to rush through.

"Slow down just a little."

"Are you nuts?" Ross asked, giving her a sideways glance.

"No. Slow down, but don't stop." She shivered. "I'm willing to yank their chains a bit, but I don't want the tables reversed."

As Ross tapped on the brakes, she lowered her window and leaned her head out, offering her best Princess Grace wave.

"Sweeties, you must be hot and famished waiting out here. Take it from me, we're happy," she called as Ross took the corner. Turning around, she beamed back at the group, calling, "Blissfully, blissfully happy!"

She was laughing as she rolled the window up and settled into her seat again.

Ross's lips twitched, then lifted into a wry grimace. "You're laying things on a bit thick, don't you think?"

"Not at all. Let them believe what they like. Heaven only knows they'll print what they like."

"True enough." Ross glanced into the mirror and swore. "Unfortunately, your little performance has been like scattering kibble to the hounds."

"What do you mean?"

"A few of them are giving chase."

She looked behind her, then hurriedly pinned a smile on her face. "I can't believe this is happening."

"I think they sense that something is up. Maybe they've guessed that we're heading for the children."

"And there's nothing they would like to film more than a shot of the sisters being reunited." She groaned, sinking down in her seat as far as her safety belt would allow.

Ross patted her knee. "Relax. They probably would have followed us anyway. Hold on."

In a heartbeat Ross made a right turn and another left. Soon he was driving with the finesse of a London cabby—quick turns, doubling back, driving down back alleys and surging onto the Interstate.

"It's working," Cara said in delight as she watched the stream of vehicles beginning to lessen.

"What time are we supposed to be at the park?"

"Polly is bringing Heidi and Zoe to the park at noon, and Melba is bringing Becca and Brianne at quarter past."

A glance at the clock assured Cara that they were well ahead of schedule, despite their mad dash through the greater Salt Lake area.

Finally, after exiting the freeway, then circling around to catch the next on-ramp, Ross offered a triumphant cry. "That's the last of them."

The Mom Squad van wove in and out of cars, and Cara found herself studying his hands. He had long, slender fingers. Artist's fingers. Surgeon's fingers. A shiver of anticipation skittered up her spine. What would it be like to be caressed by those fingers? How long would she have to wait?

Cara all but gasped at the thought. What had

come over her? When had she begun to think of making love to this man as a matter of course? Something that wouldn't happen in a matter of months or years but...

Days?

She took a deep breath to clear her head. *Think of the children...the children...*

"Nervous?" Ross asked.

Cara focused on the way her fingers were twisting the hem of her shirt in her lap and she immediately laced her fingers together. "I don't know how the girls are going to react. It will be shocking for them at the very least. I can't even imagine what it would be like to see someone who looked exactly like me."

"The psychologist told us to treat things as low-key as possible, then let the children explore the situation as they would any other curiosity. Dr. Egstrom will be there to help smooth things over."

She gripped her hands together until her knuckles turned white. Could she help it if she was a nervous person? A worrier? Would she forever be on her guard in case Ross read her thoughts? Or would she finally trust him enough to reveal her true feelings?

"It sounds so easy in theory, but in fact..."

Ross reached over to take her hands, shaking them until she loosened her grip. "We'll take things as they come. And any problems the girls might encounter can't be any worse than the alternative. It would be far more hurtful to never let them know they were twins.''

Cara knew Ross was right, but that didn't lessen her nervousness. ''Maybe we were hasty in marrying so soon. Maybe we should have introduced them to one another a little at a time?''

''But won't the girls feel more secure being together as they get acquainted? Wouldn't it be worse to be introduced to your twin, then just when your curiosity is at its highest, have her taken away time and time again?''

''I suppose.'' She bit her lip, suddenly wishing that the introductions had already taken place. She was so anxious that things go well.

Cara's heart gave a leap of joy when Ross pulled to a stop in front of the park and she saw that Heidi and Zoe were already playing near the swings. She'd been away from them for less than a day, yet she hadn't realized how much she could miss them in even that short amount of time.

''Cara!''

''Mommy!''

The twins raced toward her, their arms outstretched, their faces alight with expectation.

Cara jumped from the car before it could completely stop. ''Hello, hello!''

Both of the children were speaking at once, filling her in on everything that had happened in her absence. The meaning of their words wasn't always entirely clear, but Cara didn't mind. Wrapping her arms around them, she tried to hug them close, but they quickly squirmed away and tugged her in the direction of the swings.

"Push us!" Zoe shouted.

"We needs t'get on the swing right now," Heidi informed her good-naturedly.

"Wait a minute, you need to say hello to Ross."

The twins glanced at Ross as he strode toward them. He made an impressive sight in his carefully tailored suit. Impressive and formidable.

But instead of showing their usual exuberance, the children went behind Cara, shielding themselves with her body.

"Come on, you don't need to hide. Ross is—" she halted, then said, "—we're going to live with Ross from now on. He's going to help me take care of you. He's going to be your new daddy."

The statement didn't seem to reassure them. If anything it made matters worse. They huddled even closer, Zoe trying to climb up her leg, crying, holding her arms out to be held.

Kneeling on the ground, Cara tried to calm them. She patted their backs, coaxed them toward the swings, offered sweet words of comfort in an effort to reassure them. But they continued to glare at Ross and back away from him as if he were a frightening monster.

"Ross, maybe we should wait and have Mrs. Graves bring your children a little later."

But no sooner had she said the words than another Mom Squad van pulled into the parking place. Since Grace had volunteered to collect Mrs. Graves and the twins, Ross turned and strode toward the car.

"I'll head them off at the pass."

But he didn't have the chance. The children burst from the rolling door and raced toward him. Before Ross could stop the girls, they came running down the hill, then skidded to a stop, obviously catching their first sight of Cara's children.

For long moments the park was eerily silent as the two sets of twins stared at one another. Cara bit her lip to still her instinctive cry at the first glimpse of them together. Two little redheads. Two strawberry-blondes.

Amazing. Absolutely amazing.

Heidi was the first to move. Her brows creased in a scowl as she stepped toward Brianne. Then, without warning, she was launching herself toward her identical twin, pulling at her hair, kicking, scratching.

"Heidi, stop!"

Cara dodged toward the pair to separate them. In a heartbeat, Brianne's cries of distress were joined by Becca's as Zoe tackled her to the ground and sat on her stomach.

"Stop it. Stop it!" Cara cried, trying to grab Heidi's flailing arms.

Ross scooped Zoe off Becca while Polly and Mrs. Graves finally managed to wrestle Brianne away from Heidi's grip. The children's cries dissolved into sobs of anger and fear.

Cara looked frantically around the park. Where was the doctor? He was supposed to be here to help. He was supposed to tell them the best way to handle the situation.

Her own throat tightened with tears as Heidi turned and wrapped her arms around Cara's neck, sobbing piteously.

"I don't like her, I don't like her," the little girl screamed again and again until her voice was barely recognizable. "Make 'em go 'way! Make 'em go 'way!"

Frantic, Cara met Ross's gaze, a horrible heaviness tugging at her heart.

Had they done the wrong thing? They had thought that being near one another would comfort the children. Were they wrong in that assumption?

Zoe kicked at Ross until he released her, then

she ran to Cara, clutching at Heidi as if she feared that her sister would disappear into thin air.

Blinking at her own tears, Cara hugged them close.

"Shh...it's all right," she whispered. "Everything's all right."

But even she had trouble believing the worn-out platitudes.

Chapter Eleven

Cara rubbed her aching temples with the heels of her hands and closed the door to the twins' new bedroom.

She never wanted to go through anything like that again. It had been hours since the meeting in the park, and during that time one or another of the children had been hysterical. Nothing Cara or Ross said or Dr. Egstrom could offer managed to calm them down.

She looked up to find Ross slouched in the only piece of adult-size furniture to be found in the nursery's play area—a love seat that he still managed to dwarf.

A sob burst from her throat. "We've scarred their psyches forever."

She didn't even hesitate when he opened his arms. Sinking onto the couch beside him, she allowed him to pull her close. He hugged her to his chest while he stroked her hair in silent comfort.

"It's not that bad."

"The whole thing has been horrible. Horrible!"

"Shh."

He drew her even more securely into his embrace, tucking her head beneath his chin. Still stroking her hair, he whispered a litany of words that had no real meaning but were simply offered to comfort her. And bit by bit, as the steady beat of his heart marked the time and the warmth of his body seeped into her own, she began to believe that things would improve. Somehow.

"The children aren't scarred for life, Cara. I don't even think it's a case of their being all that shocked by discovering they each have an identical twin. I think the root of their distress lies in the simple fact that they've been confronted with a huge change to their usual routines and surroundings. Added to that is the fact that each of the twins must be feeling a sense of competitiveness and possessiveness."

"Competition? For what?"

"My children are feeling threatened that I will begin to spend time with your kids, and I'm sure Heidi and Zoe are equally possessive of your time and attention. Our situation isn't really all that different from what it would have been if each of us had brought home a new baby from the hospital. The scope of the problem from their end is simply larger because the time they had to prepare for the meeting was smaller and the 'new siblings' are their own age. Add to that the fact that each of the girls is seeing a mirror image—'' he shrugged beneath her ''—it has to have scared them.''

Cara took a deep, shuddering breath and wiped the tears from her cheeks. Looking at things from Ross's point of view, she could see the challenges involved. But as he said, she didn't see anything that could prove permanently damaging to the children's well-being. ''I suppose you're right.''

''I'm not saying that things are going to be perfect overnight. It may be months before they truly accept one another.''

She closed her eyes in horror. Could she endure even another day like the one she'd just had?

''But at least neither of us will have to survive the tantrums and emotional outbursts alone. We'll have each other to help weather the storms.''

They were a pair now. Partners. A married couple.

For the first time, she felt as if they were a married couple. She wouldn't go so far as to say they were newlyweds. But the embrace they shared had a certain familiarity about it that was reassuring.

"Are you reconsidering your stand on the nanny?" Ross asked, his voice rumbling in her ear.

She grimaced. "I feel like a failure admitting that I need help."

"Cara, even the Mom Squad Day Care wouldn't allow four three-year-olds to be supervised full-time by one adult."

"Yes, but they're *my* children."

"And if you'd given birth to all four at once, you would have neighbors and church women rallying around you to help ease the workload. Why won't you let me supply you with one little ol' nanny?"

She grimaced, knowing that she couldn't let her pride get in the way of this issue. She needed help. Maybe once the children were better acquainted with one another, things would be different. But after the day she'd had today, she was ashamed to admit she would consider the full-time services of the National Guard if it were offered. "Okay. I'll take a little old nanny, but that's it."

She pressed her hands against her eyes. She was so tired of worrying. So tired of struggling. "We've got a problem, though. After today I think Mrs. Graves is reconsidering her position as your employee. When she left, she made it quite clear that four children were too much for her to handle, as well. That means finding someone else." Before

Ross could offer any suggestions, she hurriedly added, "And I won't be shown up in my mothering skills by an au pair who is half my age, so don't even think about hiring a nanny fresh out of high school."

"We'll find someone. Don't worry." He squeezed her shoulders. "I've got connections to a magical service called the Mom Squad. I'm sure they can find us another nanny. Maybe something British along the Mary Poppins line, with a little magic up her sleeve."

Cara offered a soft snort. "Even Mary Poppins would serve notice after a day like today."

She thought Ross's lips brushed against her hair. "There's always tomorrow, Cara. And the day after that. Things will get better."

She clung to that thought with every ounce of hope she had left.

Yes. Things would get better. Time had a way of healing so many things. Fear, anger...

Grief.

Ross shifted, and Cara felt her cheeks grow warm when she realized that she still lay with her head against his chest. But when she would have moved, Ross silently urged her to remain.

The peace of the room slipped around them like velvet, easing the tension from her shoulders. She closed her eyes, concentrating on Ross's fingers stroking her hair. The sensation was heavenly and, oh, so relaxing, threatening to send her to sleep.

"Stibbs will be back tomorrow. I'll formally introduce the two of you before I leave for work, then you and he can work out the details of how you want the house run."

"Fine." Lethargy stole through her like a silken tide.

"I would like it if you'd keep your evenings free, however. At least once or twice a week I'm required to attend some sort of social gathering, and as my wife, I'll need you to accompany me."

Cara's eyes flickered, then opened as she stared unseeingly at a point in midair. Her heart squeezed with a viselike pressure.

If Ross only knew how those words echoed those that Elliot had offered her soon after their wedding. It wasn't until then that she'd realized that her role in Elliot's life was to look perfect, act perfect and organize the most perfect parties.

"We'll have to throw one or two of our own dinner parties, as well," Ross continued.

Cara felt a chill invade her limbs. This couldn't be happening. She couldn't have allowed herself to be sucked back into the same gilded trap.

"We'll keep things small until you know everyone."

Or until she knew who the "right" people were.

Her throat grew tight with tears, but this time they weren't on behalf of the children. This time they were for herself. Because she was a fool—a complete and utter fool. After managing to divorce Elliot and escape from a life that had left her feeling hollow and bleak, she had gone completely full circle again with the same kind of life and the same kind of man.

Knowing that she had to leave before she burst into tears again, she jumped to her feet and offered a choked, "Good night, Ross. I'm afraid I'm coming down with a headache, so I'll just…good night."

Then she rushed out the door, snapping it shut behind her.

ROSS STARED AT THE DOOR, hearing Cara's feet run across the hall, then the second soft thump as she closed herself in her room.

What had just happened here? He'd been so sure that he'd managed to reassure Cara about the children, the nanny, even Stibbs's role as her employee. She'd lain against him so peacefully. For long moments he'd been enveloped in a sense of contentment and well-being. Then, without warning, she'd stiffened and all but run from the room.

What had he done?

What had he said?

Thinking back, he couldn't remember anything that could have caused her sudden retreat.

"Damn." Sighing, he leaned forward, resting his elbows on his knees. Wearily he ran his fingers through his hair, hoping to ease the tension that had gripped him since the twins' arrival at the park. Despite his matter-of-fact explanation for the day's events to Cara, he hadn't been unaffected by the plight of the children. It had torn him apart to see Becca and Brianne crying and reaching out to him. Although they had gradually forgotten their mother, Ross still remembered those first awful days after Nancy's death when they'd begged him to find her and bring her home.

Today they'd fallen back into those same behaviors. It was clear they felt threatened by the presence of a new mother and two new siblings. They were clearly terrified by the sudden change in their lives, and the new trauma brought back the pain surrounding Nancy's disappearance from their lives.

Ross shuddered at the memory of his children's grief. He tried not to spoil his children, but he had made it a point to keep them emotionally sheltered.

Until now. Today he had unwittingly tested his children to the limits of their endurance.

Too weary to dwell on that point, Ross snapped off all but a night-light and made his way down the hall to the master bedroom. Once there, he stripped off his clothes. But even a hot shower didn't ease the knots in his shoulders. He was tired. Bone tired. The kind of weariness that went straight to the soul. And there wasn't a thing he could do about it. No amount of sleep would ease the exhaustion of his spirit.

And yet...

Today, during their mad dash to lose the reporters—and those quiet moments on the couch before Cara had run away—he'd been happy. His mind had been still, his body rejuvenated.

Frowning, Ross flipped off the shower and wrapped himself in a towel. Padding through the darkened bedroom, he opened one of the windows to catch the night's breeze, then flipped back the covers.

For long moments he stared at the emptiness that greeted him. Would he ever get used to sleeping alone?

As if out of habit, he glanced at the photograph of his wife on the nightstand. But for once the picture didn't offer him any answers. It was a picture, not a human being. Even the slightly self-deprecating tilt to her lips seemed to urge him to admit that talking to Nancy in his mind and clinging to the memories with a stranglehold wouldn't bring her back.

And for the first time in as long as he could remember, that thought wasn't as devastating as he had supposed it would be.

He'd loved Nancy. He would always love her. But she had always been filled with such love and laughter that she wouldn't want him to live his life as a memorial of her death.

A memorial of her death?

Was that what he'd been doing?

The strength drained from his knees, and he sank onto the edge of the bed.

Even as he inwardly protested his sudden epiphany, Ross realized that for the longest time he had focused on Nancy's rapidly developing cancer and those last painful months. He'd focused on his grief and the emptiness of his home. In doing so, he'd forgotten the love and laughter she'd inspired.

Until Cara had reminded him how good it felt to smile.

Ross picked up the frame, caressing his wife's lips with his thumb. For long moments he gazed at her face, remembering the good times they'd had together, the home they'd created and the little girls they'd loved.

Then he opened the drawer, intent on putting her inside—but hesitated.

Not tonight. In the morning he would put the

picture away—if only for a little while. But not tonight.

Tonight he would say goodbye to his memories.

Then it would be time to move on.

IN THE DAYS THAT FOLLOWED, Cara eased into her role as Ross's wife and the children's mother. She was formally introduced to Rupert Stibbs, Ross's British butler. To her delight she learned that Stibbs had a wicked sense of humor, a passion for opera and a penchant for American soap operas. He worked "days only and had every second Wednesday off" but he also had a soft spot for children and small animals—a plus since Ross's twins had hamsters that invariably escaped from their cages.

Just as Cara had suspected, Edna Graves offered her notice soon after the first meeting in the park. Cara, for one, was not disappointed. She found Mrs. Graves to be stern and rather forbidding. But interviewing a new nanny had proven to be unnecessary since Melba Wilson was swiftly recovering from her surgery and had expressed an interest in becoming the children's full-time nanny.

On the surface things seemed to be going well at the Gifford castle.

Seemed to be going well.

Cara sighed, knowing that she should be content. Ross was obviously happy with the way Cara had begun to run the finances and the household staff. So why couldn't she be content herself? Why did she constantly feel as if she needed to impress Ross? And what about the sensual tension between Ross and her that seemed to build a little more each day, until she was attuned to him with the intensity of a guitar string plucked by its master.

Groaning at her own inner musings, Cara hefted a laundry basket full of folded clothes against her hip. Most of the items in the basket belonged to the children, and she could have let Stibbs take them upstairs, but Cara enjoyed the task of putting tiny socks, underwear and shorts into their proper drawers. It gave her a sense of permanence that she wanted more desperately than she could have imagined.

Because she was growing to love Ross's children as quickly as she had bonded with her own.

Sighing, she made her way through the house. Once upstairs she tiptoed down the hall, her ear picking up the sound of childish bickering coming from the play area of the nursery. Today the children were spending the afternoon with Dr. Egstrom, and Cara was under strict orders to leave the psychologist and the little girls alone. Even so, she couldn't help wondering how things were going. Although the children had been together every day, they were still clearly upset over the changes made in their lives. Ross and Cara were hoping that some sessions with Dr. Egstrom would help them to see that they didn't have to fear the situation.

Slipping into Heidi and Zoe's room via the hall, Cara noiselessly restocked their clothing supply as she eavesdropped on what was happening in the playroom beyond.

It didn't take a session with Dr. Egstrom for her to know that Heidi and Zoe were still resentful about the move to a new home and the presence of Ross in their lives. All of the children were in turmoil with the new arrangements. They were clearly uncertain about their "mirror halves" and regarded each other with suspicion. After more than a week together, there were tears and tantrums as each set of twins fought for the attention of their customary parent. Heidi clung to Zoe, and Becca to Brianne even though they were obviously fascinated by the presence of a double. But that fascination seemed to prevent the bonding that Cara and Ross had so hoped would happen, and nothing seemed to budge their stubborn attitudes—not even when the twins accidentally mixed each other up. Cara could only hope that the doctor could help facilitate a childlike truce.

Closing the drawers, she tiptoed down the hall to Becca and Brianne's room, repeating her chore.

Again, she heard the low tones of Dr. Egstrom as he played with the twins, and she wished that someone could mediate in her relationship with Ross. She had already learned that living with Ross meant enduring her constant awareness of him. She was drawn to his brooding good looks, his infinite strength...

His passion.

In an effort to keep her sanity, Cara had done everything in her power to push away her attraction for Ross Gifford. She'd tried over and over to convince herself that he was too much like Elliot.

But already she'd discovered that such an argument was not entirely true. Although Ross was driven and ambitious, he aroused her in a way that her first husband never had. Moreover, her concerns that Ross would try to mold her into a trophy wife had so far proved unfounded—despite the comments he'd made to her that night in the nursery. Never once had he critiqued her clothes, her hair or her makeup. He didn't offer suggestions on how she should spend her days or ask her to run endless errands on his behalf. He seemed content to let her handle the finances and the children in the way she saw fit.

As well, there was a core of decency about him that urged her to trust him. She had no doubt that he would be faithful to her. Just as he had been faithful to Nancy.

And continued to be faithful to her beyond the grave, Cara thought with a grimace.

Closing the door to the child-size armoire, she noted that a pair of Ross's polo shirts remained in the bottom of the basket.

Padding down the hall, she let herself into the master bedroom suite, feeling like an interloper. Despite the fact that she'd been in here several times to deliver laundry and newly bought toiletries, she still looked upon this room as being Ross's "private space." She felt no more comfortable entering it than she did probing the private pain that still lingered in his soul.

Automatically her eyes darted to the bedside table where he kept a picture of Nancy, and then she frowned.

Where was the picture?

Afraid it had fallen to the floor, she set the basket on the bed, then dropped to her knees. Had Becca or Brianne been in here? Or worse, Heidi and Zoe? Heaven only knew they'd been curious about the picture of the redheaded woman who graced the walls in the hall and Becca and Brianne's room. Had they given in to that curiosity and done something to Nancy's photo?

Lifting the bedskirt, Cara peered under the bed, then under the table.

"Lost something?"

Her head jerked up with such force that she banged it against the edge of the nightstand. Her face instantly grew hot and she damned her propensity to blush. It wasn't as if she was doing anything wrong. She was merely trying to see if the missing picture had been damaged or fallen.

But that didn't make her feel any less guilty.

Cara scrambled to her feet, wiping her hands down the legs of her jeans—then wished she hadn't. The betraying gesture made her feel even guiltier.

"I, uh, didn't see your wife's picture...and I...thought the children might have pushed it...off the edge."

She wasn't sure, but she thought she saw a sparkle of something akin to amusement in Ross's eyes.

Great. She *had* made a fool of herself.

"I put it away."

Of all the things she had expected Ross to say, the reality took her completely by surprise.

"Beg pardon?" Again, she could have kicked herself for the betraying whisper.

"Nancy has passed away, and I have a new

wife. Don't you think that your picture should be the only one on my bedside table?"

"No. I...I mean—"

Ross chuckled and she was shocked by the sound. She had never heard anything even resembling laughter from Ross. She wasn't entirely sure she liked the way it made her stomach flutter with excitement and her knees grow weak.

Ross had paused in the doorway, but he continued on to his walk-in closet, his eyes trained on his cuff links. Cara couldn't help herself. She trailed after him like a devoted puppy.

"We'll have to get your picture taken," he said offhandedly.

"Yes—I mean, no!"

He chuckled again, and she leaned against the doorjamb for support.

She had always thought that Ross was handsome—and there was no doubt that he could inspire a white-hot passion within her with the most casual of caresses. But hearing him laugh was more potent than anything she'd experienced yet.

"Damn it. Can you help me with these things?"

Before she could gather her wits, he was holding his cuffs in her direction. With fingers that trembled, she threaded the gold studs through the buttonholes, releasing the starched fabric from his wrists. Strong wrists that could have been fashioned from stone by Michelangelo himself.

Now she was getting totally out of hand.

"How are things coming with the doctor? Any progress?"

Since he apparently wished to talk to her, Cara lingered in the doorway—even though it was apparent that Ross intended to undress.

"It's hard to say with the door closed," she said as she watched him drop the cuff links on a silver tray and begin unfastening the front of his shirt. "I hear noises, and the doctor's voice every now and then, but not enough to gather any conclusions."

"What kind of noises?"

"Nothing promising. Shrieks and shouts for the most part."

Ross grimaced. Shrugging from his shirt, he tossed it in the clothes hamper.

Cara's throat grew instantly dry. She had suspected that Ross was lean and athletically built, but she'd had no idea that his clothes hid such wide shoulders, taut pecs and a washboard stomach. She vaguely wondered when Ross found the time to work out with his already hectic schedule.

"We're going to need to throw a party sometime soon. How's the end of the month?"

She blinked and stared at him, having only caught a smattering of what he'd said.

"Beg pardon?"

"A party. Word of my marriage has leaked out, and I need to introduce you to some of my colleagues and clients. How would the end of the month work for you?"

"I—" She was suddenly awash in memories of her life with Elliot. He'd wanted nothing more than a beautiful hostess for his parties. He'd told her how to act, how to talk, how to dress. When she'd tried to develop her own ideas on the subject, he'd flown into a rage, telling her that she was his "social representative" and he wouldn't have her reflecting badly on him or his business.

If she'd only known then that he'd had an entirely different philosophy regarding the kind of woman he wanted in his bed, she might have suspected that he was keeping a mistress. As it was, she had played his game for years before discovering that she was nothing more to Elliot than a life-size doll to dress up and manipulate to his will.

"What kind of party would you like me to organize?"

"I'll take care of that."

"Oh." She was secretly hurt. Didn't he trust her judgment where his friends were concerned? "Would you like me to send out the invitations?"

"My secretary will handle that. I'll even arrange for some suitable clothes to be delivered so you won't have to worry about your wardrobe. All I need is for you to be your usual beautiful and charming self.''

Cara felt as if ice water were running through her veins.

Ross couldn't possibly know that he was reliving a scene she'd endured countless times before, but her heart ached nonetheless. She had been so sure that her life would be different with Ross. She'd thought that she would be able to fashion a place for herself in Ross's life. But after only a week of marriage, she was discovering that she was once again a trophy wife with no purpose other than to make Ross's life more comfortable.

Her throat squeezed tight with unshed tears. Why had she convinced herself that she could make a difference, that she could form an emotional bond with him? It seemed she wouldn't even be allowed to try. Stibbs ran the castle, and a nanny took care of the children. An accountant could have easily handled those responsibilities that Cara had been given.

But wasn't an accountant exactly what she was?

Her mouth grew dry. Why had she thought she could be anything more?

''Is something wrong?''

Ross was watching her, obviously waiting for a response, so she shook her head.

"No. Not a thing. The party sounds fine. Just let me know if there's anything I can do to help."

Then, before she could burst into tears, she turned on her toe and hurried out of the room.

Chapter Twelve

Perhaps it was childish, but when it became clear that she had no real place in Ross's life, Cara decided the time had come to assert herself. She would *not* become a life-size Barbie to be dressed and paraded in front of Ross's friends. She had enough pride and belief in herself to know that she had a great deal to offer this marriage if only she were given the chance.

But Cara was also wise enough to know that she would never be offered anything more than what she had unless she made it clear that she expected more of this marriage—and of Ross.

Her first show of independence was to inform Mrs. Graves that the children would no longer be requiring her services. The woman had been intent on working through her two-week notice, but she was so curt with the children that Cara felt they

would be better off without her help. Although
Melba Wilson was still far from ready to work full-
time, the older woman had stated she was eager to
see the children three times a week for a few hours
each time. Cara had jumped at the offer.

Mrs. Graves was clearly alarmed by the fact that
Cara intended to watch the children herself most
of the time. Her self-righteousness merely made
Cara more determined to do what she knew was
right. Yes, it would be a challenge to watch all of
the children at once. Yes, Cara was more than
aware of the fact that she didn't have Mrs.
Graves's formal training. But as far as Cara was
concerned, she loved the children and that was far
more important than a degree in child develop-
ment.

Last of all Cara decided that something needed
to be done about the house. Granted, it was beautiful—but it was also too elegant, opulent and overwhelming for everyday living.

Since Ross had offered her a more-than-healthy
stipend and a generous budget for household expenses, she visited a former Mom Squad employee
who had just opened her own decorating business.
Within an hour Cara was poring over paint chips
and wallpaper books. By the end of the day, a team
of painters had invaded the house with promises

that all of the changes would be finished well before the party in three weeks.

Despite her show of bravado, Cara was a nervous wreck by the time Ross came home. She had imagined every reaction he could offer from rage to annoyance to gratitude. But what she hadn't prepared herself to encounter was indifference. Complete and total indifference.

She was waiting for him in the kitchen when he walked in. It was late, and the children had given up and gone to bed nearly an hour earlier.

Ross looked tired. His shoulders had lost some of their proud line, and weariness etched grooves on either side of his mouth.

"Bad day in court?"

He grimaced. "Worse. A divorced couple came into the office to divvy up their possessions. The two of them nearly came to blows a couple of times."

The thought of divorced couples divvying up their worldly belongings made her distinctly uncomfortable, so she said instead, "I've got dinner for you."

Aren't you being the traditional wifey, a little voice inside her chided. Normally Cara couldn't think of anything worse than cooking. But since it was Stibbs's day off, she'd wanted to put him into the best frame of mind possible.

"You're a lifesaver. I'll just go upstairs and shower."

"No!"

His brows rose at her vehement outburst. Then his eyes narrowed in suspicion, and she realized that she wouldn't be given the opportunity to break the news to him gently.

"Now, I don't want you to freak out," she began quickly.

He took a deep breath. "What have they done?"

"They?" He couldn't possibly know about the painters already.

"The children."

"Oh, no. They haven't done anything. Actually, I think they're beginning to get used to one another. Today I managed to convince them to go on a picnic at the park. They played on the swings with one another and took turns on the slide and the merry-go-round—"

She pressed her lips together, realizing that she was close to babbling.

"What's happened?"

"Nothing is wrong, per se, and you did tell me that I could make some changes to the house if I felt like it."

He eyed her for long minutes. "Within reason."

Within reason? What did that mean? A few new

pillows? Or whatever she wanted, barring major construction?

Ross sighed. ''Maybe you'd better show me what you've done.''

Cara threaded her fingers together. ''Okay. Follow me.''

She took him into the front living room—a huge cavernous space that she and the painters had nicknamed The Great Hall. Most of the furniture had been moved out of the room, but those items that remained had been covered with drop cloths. What was most evident of all, however, was that the walls had already been altered—from the original stark white to a pale petal-pink.

Cara loved the transformation. The room suddenly seemed more intimate and warm. The rich color complemented the warm tones of the wood, allowing the beauty of the carvings to take center stage. Cara could already see the finished product in her mind's eye—new throw pillows in a variety of colors and textures, artwork with bold themes, splashes of color with fresh plants and objets d'art from both Ross's and her own collections.

''I painted,'' she finally said, stating the obvious. Then she nibbled her thumbnail and looked to see how Ross was reacting.

''Why?''

She wasn't sure what she had expected, but that question wasn't it.

"The white is too stark and…off-putting."

She saw the muscle of his jaw working.

"My former wife designed the house."

Oh-oh. She'd treaded on sacred ground. Nevertheless the answer explained a lot. She'd had a hard time connecting the elaborate nature of the house with Ross's innate reserve and love for order.

"The castle is very beautiful," she said slowly, "but the stark white makes it look so…sterile."

The muscle jumped again.

"Don't you think you should have asked me first?"

Cara took a deep breath. This was one argument that she had anticipated. "Perhaps. But I ventured out on my own to prove a point."

She rushed on before he had a chance to respond. "I don't know what you expected when you married me, Ross, but there are a few things that we need to get straight right here and now." Summoning all of her courage, she plunged ahead. "I am not your first wife—"

"I didn't say you were."

"No, but I want it made clear that I don't intend to take her place."

"I never intimated that I wanted you to."

"No, you haven't. But I need you to acknowledge that I won't look like her, act like her or attempt to be like her in any way."

"Have I ever indicated that you should?"

"Yes!" The resentment she'd held within her burst free. "We married in order for me to take her place as your children's mother. But since my arrival, it has become clear that you don't trust me with the job—or any of the other duties around here. You have a butler to run your household, a nanny to take care of the children, a gardener to see to the yard. You have a cleaning service and a grocery delivery service. You have a maid and a psychologist."

"The arrangements are practical."

"The arrangements make me obsolete in your life."

"There are other things—"

"Like what? You stated once that I would help you entertain, but you've already made it clear that you will take care of everything in that department, too. You've planned a party, but rather than let me feel useful in some small way, you've already arranged for a local service to plan everything from the menu to the invitations. You've even chosen what clothes I should wear!"

She took a deep breath, then bit her lip. She

hadn't lost her temper like that in ages. But then, she supposed she was past due.

"I was married to a man like that once before, Ross. He planned my life and my daily activities from the moment I woke up until I went to bed at night. He decided what I would wear, what I would eat and what friends I would have."

Her throat grew tight with emotions. "I won't live like that again, do you hear me? When I divorced Elliot, I swore that I would never allow another man that kind of power in my life. I swore that I would never marry at all."

Ross's eyes glittered. "If you were so dead set against sharing your life with another man, why did you agree to the proposition at all? Why did you agree to marry me?"

She swept her hand wide. "Look around you, look at the car you drive, the house you live in, the company you keep? How could I possibly compete against that?"

"Compete?"

"You threatened to take my children away!"

The muscle in his jaw jumped. "I never would have gone to such lengths."

"Are you so sure? You're a man who's accustomed to getting what you want—regardless of the methods."

"I'd hardly go that far."

"Be honest with yourself, Ross. Would you really have given Zoe up without a fight? Any fight that was necessary."

His jaw tightened, but he didn't speak.

"I think I have my answer," she whispered, hurt, even though she had already suspected as much. "Do you really think I would have stood a chance against that kind of determination?"

When he remained silent, she closed the distance between them, pointing an accusing finger in his direction.

"Before we go any further in this relationship, I want the record set straight. I will be an equal partner or I'll file for divorce."

Ross's eyes narrowed. Then he glanced at the walls behind her. "There will be no divorce." Then, gesturing to the pale-pink color, he said softly, "Do whatever you want. It looks nice." Then he turned and made his way back to the kitchen. "Just let me know if you plan on knocking down any walls. As for the party, check with the people I hired and make any changes you feel necessary. I was merely trying to give you some time to adjust to our arrangement before I made any demands on your time. After tonight, I'll delegate more of the details to you."

Cara stood with her mouth open, the fight draining out of her. She had been ready for a confrontation, and now it appeared she wasn't going to get one.

So why did she feel so disappointed?

What had she hoped he would do? Argue with her?

Yes.

With a sinking sensation, she realized that she craved his attention so much that she was willing to argue with him in order to get it. Was she that needy? That wanton? Was she so hungry for his touch? His attention?

Yes.

The thought was humbling as much as it was troubling. She'd prided herself on moving past a point where she felt she had to have a man in her life in order to feel complete.

But it wasn't just any man that would do....

With a sinking heart she realized that she wanted Ross and no one else. She wanted his heart as well as his attention.

Sighing, she realized that she might be asking for the moon. Ross was willing to share his home and his life with her. But his heart?

She shied away from even thinking about that. Tomorrow she would call the caterer and the party organizer and take charge of Ross's soiree. By the time she finished, he would see that she didn't intend to be a mere figurehead in their relationship. She would *make* him need her.

Turning, Cara took a deep breath and viewed the painter's progress.

Ross hadn't balked at her alterations, so the time had come to move full steam ahead. She would see if the decorator could hire some additional help to expand the scope of the remodeling. She wanted everything to be perfect when the guests arrived.

Nevertheless, she couldn't entirely still the little voice that whispered to her that her motives had less to do with making the castle a home and more to do with making Ross acknowledge that she was an integral part of his life. She wasn't an employee or a live-in nanny.

She was his wife.

"IT'S BEAUTIFUL. Absolutely beautiful."

Cara carefully studied the expressions of her friends from the Mom Squad, looking for any sign of reserve. "You really think so?"

Polly grinned. "I can't believe the transformation you've made with a little paint and wallpaper."

"Not to mention a few feminine touches," Grace added.

Cara turned to Bettina. "Any cosmic vibrations worth noting?"

"Mmm. The cosmic vibrations have been very busy during our tour." But Bettina wasn't looking at the house, she was studying Cara. "How are things going with Ross and you?"

Cara shifted uncomfortably, then motioned for her friends to take a seat. She had ended their tour at the sunroom next to the kitchen. The intimate niche had only needed a few minor changes in Cara's estimation. She'd painted the walls a soft buttery-yellow, added even more plants and potted flowers, topped the chairs with chintz cushions and framed the window with a chintz swag looped over an antique curtain rod with huge carved finials.

Once her friends were seated, she began pouring tea from a delicate antique chintz ware tea set that had belonged to Cara's mother.

"Things are fine."

Polly snorted. "Now tell us what the situation is really like."

Cara grimaced. "Complicated."

"Has he said anything about all of the remodeling you've done?" Grace asked.

"The most I've been able to get out of him is that things look 'fine.'"

The women began helping themselves to the finger sandwiches and pastries that Stibbs had elegantly arranged on a silver server.

"So he hasn't objected to the complete overhaul?'' Bettina inquired after taking a sip of herbal tea.

Cara idly stirred her own cup. "The first night we had a small...confrontation.''

The women exchanged knowing glances.

"Actually, I should probably clarify that I exploded and started telling him that I wasn't his first wife and he should stop comparing me to her.'' She took a breath at the memory, then continued. "Since then, he's been rather...distant.''

Her friends watched her with open concern.

"How are the children?" Grace finally asked.

"They're doing much better. They're beginning to play with one another. Occasionally we even find that they've sneaked into a single room to sleep for the night. It's so cute to find them all sprawled together on the same bed.''

"So Ross is the major problem on your road to bliss,'' Bettina offered.

Cara bit her lip and nodded.

"And it bothers you that you simply...coexist,'' Bettina continued.

"Yes.'' The word was small and infinitely telling, even to her own ears.

Grace took her hand. "Have you fallen in love with him?"

"No, of course not. I simply need to feel... needed and—'' She stopped, her throat growing tight with tears. When she caught her friends' concerned looks, she had to admit the truth to herself.

She *had* fallen in love with her own husband.

And her worst fear was that he couldn't—or wouldn't—love her back.

CARA DRESSED CAREFULLY for the party the following night, knowing that the evening was an important one. Not only would her efforts as a hostess be scrutinized, but she was also about to be introduced to Ross's friends and colleagues.

As his wife.

From deep in the house Cara heard the doorbell ring. A quick glance at the clock on her bedside table assured her that it was early for guests to be arriving, so someone must be incredibly early.

She had to admit that, as much as she'd dreaded the party, she was actually looking forward to it. She'd made sure that Ross's guest list was augmented with a few invitees of her own. Grace, Polly and Bettina would be there, as well as Dr. Egstrom and his wife.

Cara had prepared carefully for the event. She'd delegated the painting to the decorator, then had enlisted Stibbs's help in planning the perfect party.

It hadn't been at all surprising to her that he had a flair for entertaining. Nor did it particularly surprise her that Ross had never known that fact. He'd always turned such events over to a professional party planner, assuming that Stibbs wouldn't want to work past his normal hours.

But Stibbs had been delighted. Before Cara quite knew what had happened, he'd arranged for a string quartet, called the caterers and the decorators.

And tonight would be perfect.

Crossing to the windows, Cara drew aside the curtain and gasped. In the late shadows the back terrace glittered like a fairyland. Tiny lights twinkled from every bush and tree. The pool was afloat with votive candles. Flowers and clinging vines graced the tables and every possible niche.

Surely Ross would have to be impressed.

Cara's stomach flip-flopped with nerves. She'd spent the morning with the twins, playing games and baking cookies. Then she'd turned the children over to Melba so that Cara could spend the rest of the day preparing for the party.

Turning, Cara gazed at her reflection in the full-length mirror, barely recognizing herself. It had been so long since she'd dressed in anything but "mom attire."

At Grace's suggestion she'd gone to a spa for the works—manicure, pedicure, facial and a complete makeover. Her hair had been trimmed and feathered away from her face in a manner that was both dramatic and waifish. Her eyes and bone structure had been highlighted with a careful application of makeup, and her dress…

She had to give Polly credit for the dress. The two of them had gone shopping earlier that week. And while Cara had been leaning toward a simple black sheath, Polly had talked her into buying a gown that was a shocking scarlet.

Cara smoothed the fabric, twisting this way and that. From the front the dress gave an illusion of demureness with a bateau neckline and a bias cut that clung to her figure before swirling around her feet. But from the rear…

Twisting, she grinned when she caught sight of the expanse of bare flesh. The dress had a drape of fabric that rested low on her hips, while above, there was nothing but a naked expanse of skin.

Perhaps she shouldn't have been so bold, but she'd always had a flare for the dramatic—one that Elliot had never allowed her to express. So when Polly had insisted that the black sheath was too predictable for the evening, Cara had hesitated, wondering if the red dress might help her prove to Ross that she wasn't nearly as biddable as he'd thought she might be. Nor was she prepared to blend into the woodwork.

A soft tap disturbed her musings, and Cara's

heart leaped. Without being told, she knew who waited on the other side of the panels. And she also knew that the moment Ross saw her, the die would be cast. Either he would be dismayed by her audacity...

Or maybe, just maybe, he would finally see her as a woman who was more than just a mother.

Chapter Thirteen

"Cara, are you ready? Our guests are beginning to arrive."

Our guests. The inclusive pronoun gave Cara the impetus she needed to cross the room and open the door.

"Yes, I'm ready."

For long minutes she was greeted with silence as Ross's gaze slid from her waifish haircut to the tips of her toes.

"You look beautiful."

His eyes had grown dark and heated. The way he stared at her made her feel as if she was the only woman on earth.

"Thank you."

Ross was devastating, as well. He had dressed in a tuxedo, and she wondered idly if it was the same tuxedo he'd worn the night she'd met him.

So much had changed since their first encounter—and not just with their marriage and the children. Cara felt as if she were a different person. Stronger in so many ways and yet still so weak where Ross was concerned. So needy.

She shivered beneath his regard, soaking up the blatant desire than radiated from his gaze.

"So beautiful," he murmured again.

A frisson of delight sped down her spine, and she felt her pulse skip a beat. For a moment there were no ghosts between them, only pure, honest regard....

As well as a heady, unspoken awareness.

From far below, the doorbell rang again.

"Shouldn't we go down?" she prompted softly.

Ross's lips lifted in a smile, and she was shaken to her toes with the effect it had in softening his features. She was suddenly aware of the fact that she was seeing that smile more and more often. Could she dare to think that she was making a difference in his life? That she was helping him to forget the past and be happy?

Another peal of the doorbell caused his smile to fade into a grimace.

"It seems we won't be given any more time to ourselves." Ross offered her his arm. "Shall we?"

Nodding, she allowed him to escort her down the hall.

"The house and the grounds are beautiful. You've obviously been hard at work, Cara."

His praise warmed her as much as his earlier regard. "Thanks. Everyone has been working hard."

"But I'd bet you did the lion's share." She felt his gaze upon her again as Ross continued, "Yet you still found time to tend to the children and see to my comfort as well."

Ross stopped her short of the staircase so that they were still hidden from prying eyes.

"I never meant to hurt you by excluding you from the preparations. I merely thought—"

She placed her fingers over his lips. "I know."

Ross smiled. "If I'd known that you would be such a stupendous hostess, I never would have dreamed of interfering." His tone softened, becoming low and intimate. "I seem to discover something new about you every day." He touched her cheek, then stroked the line of her jaw. "You never cease to surprise me."

She grimaced. "I doubt there are many surprises left. I'm really a simple person."

Ross shook his head. "No, you're a complex mix—wife, mother, girl next door." His hand touched her back and he grew suddenly still. "Turn around."

She felt herself flushing, knowing that he'd been

so intent on studying the front of her gown that he hadn't noticed there was no back to speak of.

Holding the slight train out of the way, she pivoted on her toe, slowly, tantilizingly. Then she looked up to see his reaction.

Ross's eyes flared with an instantaneous passion.

"What have you done?"

She shook her head in confusion, wondering if she'd offended him by being so bold in front of his guests.

But Ross merely slipped his hand around her waist, his fingers dipping beneath the edge of the satin drape.

"I've got hours before I'll have you alone again," he whispered. "Hours and hours."

Then he leaned down to kiss her, softly at first, then more and more intimately until both of them were gasping for breath. When he finally drew free, there was no doubt in her mind that he approved of her choice in attire.

"You'll need to add *seductress* to your list of qualifications," he whispered against her ear.

Cara gasped at the flurry of sensation inspired by his breath caressing her hair.

"I'm no seductress," she said softly as his hand spread wide, moving in slow circles against her back.

"You are in that dress."

She rested her hands at his waist when her knees threatened to buckle.

"If we didn't have guests downstairs," Ross said with patent regret, "I wouldn't let you out of my arms." He leaned toward her again, his lips grazing her hair, her cheek, her throat.

Her hands slid around his waist to draw him even closer. He'd been avoiding her ever since Nancy's picture had disappeared from his nightstand. But the hunger of his embrace, the firm pressure of his lips pressing against her own left her in no doubt that he'd been thinking about her.

Wanting her.

"The party," she whispered, hearing the murmur of voices floating up the staircase.

Ross pulled her tightly against him, tucking her head beneath his chin. "Just say the word and I'll send them all home."

Even though she knew the option was impractical, Cara was tempted. But she didn't give in to her baser yearnings. Instead, she stepped away, smoothing the fabric of her dress.

"We can't do that." She was stunned by the hunger evident in her own voice.

Ross touched her lips with his thumb, then took a deep, shuddering breath.

"I suppose not. You've gone to too much trouble to make the evening perfect."

But as his hand slid to the hollow of her back, and he ushered her to the stairs, he leaned close to whisper in her ear, "There's always later."

AS THE FIRST OF THE GUESTS began to offer their goodbyes, Ross felt a deep satisfaction warm him from within. The evening had been a rousing success from beginning to end. His associates had been impressed by the preparations and bowled over by Cara's charm. She'd been the perfect asset to Ross, making newcomers feel welcome and old friends feel cherished. She'd laughed when confronted with the latest stories about the twins that were being bandied about on the news and in the tabloids, then she'd skillfully guided the conversation to other topics. She'd been so at ease and captivating, Ross was sure that most of the people who attended would soon be spreading the word that the Giffords had a love match.

Through it all Ross had soon discovered that he no longer cared what his associates thought or the media reported. His one and only concern lay in what Cara was thinking and feeling.

She was so beautiful.

So alive.

More and more Ross was beginning to see that he'd been living in a fog for far too long. He'd been numbly sleepwalking through his job and his role as a father. He'd gone through the motions, doing what was expected of him but little more.

Until now. He suddenly found himself hungry for life.

And love.

The thought frightened him more than he would ever have thought possible. Hadn't he vowed to remain emotionally detached? Hadn't he promised himself that this marriage of convenience would be based on mutual respect and little else? Hadn't he sworn that he wouldn't let his emotions become involved?

So when had he stopped listening to the inner warnings for caution? When had he begun to look upon his relationship with Cara as being more than a convenience?

His gaze clung to her as she circulated through the small handful of guests that still remained. She was so totally unaware of her effect on men that she made him want her all the more. She'd just about driven him crazy in that dress. He couldn't seem to keep his hand from sliding over the bare expanse of her back. Nor could he banish the image of slipping the straps from her shoulders and allowing the sensuous satin to slip to the floor.

As if she'd sensed his regard, Cara glanced over her shoulder. In that instant he caught an answering heat in her gaze and knew that the platonic aspect of their marriage wouldn't last the night.

A heat flared low in his belly, but he made no effort to banish it.

It seemed like hours before the last guest finally made his way out of the door to where the hired valet had parked the man's car. Gripping the terrace railing, Ross watched the influential judge slide into his car and drive into the dark night. He vaguely noted the distant flash of light as the reporters took yet another round of pictures.

Then the night was silent and still.

Turning his head, he found Cara waiting in the doorway.

"I've sent the catering crew home," she murmured. "Tomorrow is soon enough to clean up."

"And Stibbs?"

"He disappeared into his room. I believe he's relaxing to the sounds of *La Bohème*."

Ross pushed himself upright and walked slowly toward her. "And what about you, Mrs. Gifford? Aren't you tired?"

"I'm too keyed-up to feel it yet."

She was watching him with wide eyes, and for a moment Ross considered ending the evening here and now. She had the look of a deer caught in the headlights—too stunned to move, too fascinated to resist. But just as quickly as his chivalric instincts appeared they faded away. He needed her too much to let things end that way. He needed to touch her, hold her, caress her. He needed to reassure himself that he could still feel something in his heart other than grief, that he was still capable of loving.

Loving?

The thought hit him with the intensity of a lightning bolt. But as he drew Cara into his arms and began to kiss her—slowly at first, then with the hunger of a starving man—he knew that he had already crossed an imaginary line. He could no longer pretend to be emotionally uninvolved. Although his head warned him of the inherent dangers of caring for another woman, his heart could no longer be denied.

Forgetting the journalists with their telephoto lenses and night vision, Ross swept Cara into his arms and carried her into the house. But this time as he closed the door with his shoulder, he didn't set her down. Instead, sensing her tacit consent to his intentions, he continued up the staircase and down the hall to Cara's bedroom.

CARA WOKE TO SUNSHINE streaming through her bedroom window. Her body was deliciously lethargic and sated, and she smiled to herself, stretching luxuriously.

She couldn't remember ever feeling so wonderful, so at peace with herself and her surroundings.

Peeking beneath her lashes, she saw that she was alone in the bed. The fact didn't surprise her. Judging by the angle of the sun, it was late and she knew that Ross had been scheduled to appear in court first thing in the morning.

Turning, she reached her hand toward the pillow on the opposite side of the bed, then paused when her fingers encountered something other than fabric.

A tender smile formed on her lips when she peered through her lashes and discovered that a single rose had been left on her pillow.

In an instant her heart flooded with emotion, and she trembled from sheer, overpowering joy.

She was in love. Completely and utterly in love. And ironically, the object of her affections was her own husband.

Laughing softly to herself, she breathed deep of the rose's heavenly fragrance. The hours in Ross's arms had been beyond her wildest imaginings. He'd been passionate and tender, making her feel beautiful and desirable. Over and over again he'd brought her to the heights of ecstasy, only to hold her close in the aftermath.

So much had changed in such a short amount of time. In the space of a few hours her world had altered from one of uncertainty to one of great hope.

"We're going to make it," she whispered to herself. "Despite its beginnings, this marriage is going to be a happy one."

But by the end of the day Cara wasn't nearly so certain. She had been so sure that Ross would come home right after court, but there had been no sign of him that afternoon or at dinnertime. Finally, exhausted by the previous evening's late hours, she'd curled up on the couch in the great hall, intent on waiting for Ross there. But when she'd awakened the following morning in her own bed, she had no doubts that she had slept there alone.

She told herself that the following day would be different. She purposely chose activities that would keep her and the children close to home. But other than a few close calls with reporters trying to scale the fence, she saw no sign of anyone approaching the house.

It wasn't until she was putting laundry away in Ross's room that she received the blow that she hadn't been expecting. There on his nightstand, nearly obscured by a pile of yellow legal pads, was Nancy's picture.

The sight was so devastating that the laundry basket fell from her fingers. A sharp cry escaped her lips.

A noise behind her made her turn. There, standing on the threshold, was Ross.

She couldn't speak, couldn't move. But she realized in an instant that she didn't need to say a thing. His expression and the shadows in his eyes told her eloquently enough that he regretted their night together.

The pain was so intense she felt as if her legs would buckle. But knowing that she couldn't let him see how much he'd hurt her, she quickly scrambled to put the spilled clothes back into the hamper.

"Cara, I—"

"Give me a minute and I'll let Stibbs know that you're here."

"He already knows."

"I see. Well, I'll just go get the children. They're hungry, and I'm sure they'll be glad to know you'll be joining them for dinner."

Knowing she had to get out of there before the tears fell, she dropped the hamper on his bed, then darted toward the door. But before she could pass him, his hand shot out to grasp her elbow.

"Cara, I—"

"Don't," she whispered, the pain raw in her voice. She blinked at the moisture gathering in her eyes and pierced him with a gaze rife with accusation.

"Don't tell me that everything is all right. And don't tell me that anything has changed." A bitter laugh tripped over her lips. "I was a fool to think that making love with you had improved anything. You're still in love with a dead woman, and there's no room in your heart for me."

ROSS REELED BACKWARDS, Cara's words searing him with the intensity of a lance. But even as he would have gone after her to argue her point, he found he couldn't move.

She was right.

His eyes squeezed shut as the pain shuddered through him. Since making love to Cara, he'd been filled with so many conflicting emotions. When he'd arranged their marriage, he'd been so sure that he could slip into the role of "husband" while keeping himself emotionally aloof.

But even though he had come to a point where he had accepted Nancy's death and was ready to move on to his own future without her, he still balked at the emotional ramifications of beginning another relationship. Try as he might, he couldn't seem to banish his fears for the future. Death had stolen his happiness once before. And as much as he tried to reassure himself that fate wouldn't deal him a similar hand again, a part of him believed that the only way to avoid loving and losing was not to love at all.

It had been a mistake to make love with Cara. His eyes closed at the mere memory of the passion and delight that he'd experienced that night. He'd been transported to another world, one without pain or doubt or want.

But upon waking to find Cara nestled in his arms, he'd known that it wouldn't be fair to revel in the physical aspect of their relationship unless he could offer Cara more. She was a woman who needed to be loved, completely and wholeheartedly. And to offer her anything less would merely cheapen their relationship.

So Ross had done his best to put some space between them. He'd purposely worked longer and later. On those few occasions where he'd seen Cara, he'd done his best to appear cool and unaffected by her presence—even as his body and his heart had other ideas.

But it wasn't working. He'd thought that by giving them space, he could put some perspective on their single night of passion. Instead he found himself growing more and more hungry for her laughter, her tenderness, her passion…

And her love.

So what was he going to do? He wasn't fool

enough to think that either Cara or he could return
to an emotionless relationship.

But neither could he find the strength to allow
himself to offer her anything more.

AFTER THEIR CHANCE MEETING in Ross's bedroom,
Cara went out of her way to avoid being alone with
her husband. She concentrated her time on the children.

In that respect, at least, things were going well.
The girls were growing more and more attached to
one another. They no longer seemed to differenti-
ate between "my twin and the other twins." Instead, a palpable emotional bonding had begun to
occur—so much so, that when the reporters continued to hound her every move, Cara invited the
media to join her and the twins for playtime at a
local park. With Stibbs's help, she prepared a picnic for the reporters and cameramen, let them take
their fill of pictures and sound bites, then bade
them a fond but firm farewell.

If she'd thought that her actions might infuriate
Ross, she'd been disappointed. On one of those
rare occasions when they were in the same room
at the same time, he'd glanced at the newspapers
and magazines Stibbs had left in a pile on the
counter. After skimming the articles, his only comment had been, "The twins need a swing set of

their own. I'll have one delivered as soon as possible.''

Soon the days began to run together, one indistinguishable from the next. And Cara became haunted by her growing hunger for Ross's love. But if she'd hoped that Ross would weaken, that his iron-willed control would relax, she was doomed to disappointment.

As the weeks progressed Cara feared that the girls were beginning to pick up on the tension surrounding their parents. Attempting to allay their suspicions, she insisted that Ross accompany them to the zoo. But he remained so remote and cool, she feared that her efforts had only harmed matters more.

So when they returned from their trip and Ross abruptly left and closeted himself in his study, Cara was brought to a breaking point.

Over and over again she had tried to convince herself that she didn't need Ross's affection. But she was swiftly beginning to realize that she couldn't fool herself any longer.

She needed Ross to feel something—*anything*—for her other than remote politeness or even a hollow passion. She yearned to have him acknowledge her as a person rather than a convenience, as a partner rather than a helpmate. She needed to feel...

Needed.

Loved.

Cherished.

Still, it wasn't until she stumbled upon Ross sitting alone in his darkened study one evening that she realized she had reached a point where decisions needed to be made.

She and the children had spent most of the day with Ross. As promised, he had decided that the time had come for the girls to have their own swing set. They'd clambered into the Suburban he'd bought and made a trip to a specialty shop where the children had "test driven" every possible piece of playground equipment.

Through it all she'd sensed a lightening to his mood, a softening of the tension surrounding his mouth and the set of his shoulders. And fool that she was, she'd dared to believe that Ross had come to an emotional turning point.

Therefore, it was all the more painful when he suddenly asked, "What are your plans for the future, Cara?"

"The future?" she echoed weakly. Her heart twisted in her chest and she quipped, "Which future is that? Tomorrow or next week?"

He remained still and quiet for far too long. Cara wasn't deceived. He might slouch in his chair and stare at a spot somewhere in the darkness, but she knew his mind was working furiously.

"Our future. What exactly do you see for us? What is it that you want from this relationship?"

Her mouth grew dry, and her brain frantically scrambled for a coherent answer even as her heart broke in two. The mere mention of the years ahead of her filled her with fear. Despite her inner warnings, she had fallen in love with Ross, deeply and irrevocably. But if Ross already had doubts about the soundness of continuing their marriage—after little more than a few months—she had no illusions that there would be any happily-ever-afters for them.

She shuddered, gripping the doorjamb for strength. The most she could hope for would be a distant form of fondness or perhaps an intimate companionship. But theirs would never be a passionate joining of souls. Just as she had suspected from the beginning, Ross was incapable of offering her that kind of commitment. Indeed, if his actions over the past few weeks were anything to go by, he was already beginning to tire of her company.

Just as Elliot had done.

Was it only a matter of time before Ross began looking for another conquest?

Without warning, her temper snapped. Slapping

her hands on the woodwork, she strode toward Ross's desk.

"How should I know what I want out of our relationship? We've already crossed the line of pure convenience, and no matter how much we try to pretend otherwise, we can't go back."

She strode toward him, stabbing a finger in the air. "But I don't know if I want to go forward, either. There was a time when I would have done anything to see if we could make this…this cock-eyed marriage into something real. Then I got a full dose of what it was like to be married to the great Ross Gifford—and let me tell you, it hasn't been a picnic. You're so tied up in your own little ivory tower of grief that it's become a habit to you. Even when you seem more than ready to put your wife's death behind you and carry on with your life, you can't let go. And I think that your motives have less to do with your attachment to Nancy than with your unwillingness to take life whatever way it comes."

Cara knew that her voice was rising and that Stibbs and the children could probably hear her from the far recesses of the house. But she couldn't stop yet. Not when the words were burning to be expressed.

"Life doesn't come with any guarantees, Ross Gifford. Everyone has his or her own measure of pain to endure—and you're not the only one who has suffered. But what makes the rest of us different is that we work through our feelings and then we press on. We don't become martyrs and we don't live the rest of our lives in fear of what further calamity might befall us.''

She rested her hands on the desk, bending toward him. ''If you were to ask me, I'd say you were a coward. You have an inestimable capacity to love, but you won't allow yourself to feel anything more than the barest sense of commitment. And I'm not just talking about our relationship. Even with your own girls you offer them mere pieces of yourself.''

Ross jumped to his feet. ''I love my daughters!''

''Then show them. Show them how much they mean to you. Show them that they are the most important thing in your life and that nothing will get in the way of that—not work, not life, not even your own uncertainties for the future! They deserve that much. We all deserve that much. Especially me.''

The words echoed in the stillness of the room and Cara clapped her hands over her mouth. Dear heaven, she had done the unspeakable. She had belittled his grief and censured him for his ability to parent. Worse yet, she had all but declared her love for him. She had stripped herself bare and exposed the needy part of her that would never be happy until he loved her in return.

A sob bubbled up in her throat, and without waiting for his reply, she rushed from the room. But as she hurried up the staircase, she was suddenly aware of one demoralizing fact.

Ross had made absolutely no effort to stop her.

IT WAS LONG PAST MIDNIGHT when Ross climbed the stairs and made his way to his own room. He couldn't remember a time when he'd felt so weary, so...

Empty.

For hours he'd sat in the darkness, reviewing Cara's words time and time again. And what had shamed him most was that he had no defense.

She was right. He had made himself a martyr to his own grief. Not on behalf of his love for Nancy, but to insulate him from feeling anything that deep and overwhelming ever again.

Slowly making his way down the hall, Ross was inundated with thoughts of Cara and the way she had turned his well-ordered existence upside down. And with each step he took nearer her bedroom door, he knew that he wanted nothing more than to fall in love with her.

But if he let go of the last shreds of his resistance, he feared for the future ahead of them. If he truly loved her, if he gave her his heart and soul, could he survive losing her—to death or divorce?

He paused in front of her door, his hand resting against the panels as if he could feel her on the other side.

He knew that Cara had always entertained doubts that their marriage would last. And he had no illusions that she would leave him if she ever reached a point where she could no longer be happy.

What would he do if she left him?

How would he survive?

A hand seemed to squeeze his heart from inside his chest. For the first time he forced himself to look at how much he would lose if he couldn't give Cara what she needed most.

His love.

Immediately his heart urged him to take a chance. But, his brain…

His brain still shied away from the ramifications.

Resolutely he turned away from Cara's door. The time had come for him to do some deep soul searching. Once and for all he needed to decide just how much he was willing to offer this relationship. And to do so, it was time that he faced up to his own shortcomings.

Only then, after he'd made peace with himself and the ghosts of his past, could he approach Cara with a heart that was completely free.

Chapter Fourteen

Over the next few days Cara became keenly aware of the way that Ross went out of his way to avoid her, and she was hurt.

Was she that horrible a person? A lover? A woman? More than ever she was reminded of the circumstances surrounding their marriage. Again and again she tried to remind herself that she didn't have a right to make any emotional demands on their relationship. Theirs was a marriage of convenience, a business arrangement, a parenting partnership.

But her heart wouldn't listen. Try as she might, she couldn't seem to banish the need for a shred of fondness, companionship, devotion.

In such times she chided herself for being a fool and marrying a man who was too much like her first husband. But even that argument was beginning to wear thin. She had long ago come to the conclusion that comparing Elliot to Ross was like comparing mud to water. Yes, the two men were wealthy and powerful, but there the similarities ended. Elliot had been a user. From the beginning he had manipulated their relationship to fit his own ends without regard to her happiness. But Ross...

Was Ross so different? Hadn't he arranged their marriage to ensure the welfare of his children? Was his manipulation of the situation any less real just because it had been done on behalf of the children?

Yes, she realized. The situation was very different. Where Elliot had been concerned with nothing more than his own goals and objectives, Ross was deeply concerned about all of the children—hers as well as his. Moreover, she was beginning to see that Ross was as deeply concerned about her own happiness. He would offer her anything she wanted.

Anything but his own heart.

And therein lay the problem. Despite the fact that she had told herself she would never love again, that she would never willingly trust a man with her heart, that she would keep all of her relationships uncomplicated and based on nothing more than mutual respect and affection...

She now wanted more. So much more.

Cara bit her lip, blinking back the tears that

sprang to her eyes. Now that they had made love, they could never return to a platonic arrangement. And the thought of making love to him again without any emotional ties on his part was more painful than she ever would have imagined.

A bitter laugh tumbled from her lips. Life could be cruel at times. Just when she'd thought she had begun to follow a smooth, trouble-free existence, she had discovered that she did believe in marriage and love and commitment and all its trappings.

Which made it even harder to face the fact that Ross might never love her as much as he did Nancy.

And Cara was swiftly beginning to realize that she couldn't live in a relationship where she would always be ''second best'' in Ross's affections.

Cara huddled in the middle of her bed, her chin upon her updrawn knees, her arms wrapped around her legs.

So what was she going to do?

The early-morning sunlight slowly crept across the carpet and onto her bed, and with each inch of progress Cara's heart ached a little more.

She really had only two options. She could stay and pray that Ross's lack of affection didn't totally destroy her spirit.

Or she could leave.

And leaving Ross now would be the only way to protect herself from future pain.

Crossing to the writing desk, she withdrew her prettiest stationery. Sitting down, she began to compose her goodbye letter to Ross—all the while knowing that she was a coward for sneaking away rather than facing him in person.

"Dear Ross...it has become clear that you can never love me..."

Shaking her head, she balled up the paper and pushed it aside. She mustn't sound that pitiful and needy.

"When you find this letter, I'll be gone..."

No. It sounded like the lyrics of a Country Western song.

"Ross, you'll never know how much I've grown to love you..."

Good grief, no. She couldn't let him see how she'd allowed herself to love a man who couldn't love her back.

For nearly an hour Cara struggled to compose a letter that would offer her reasons for leaving in a way that was logical and compassionate.

Finally, forcing herself to sign her latest version—no matter how far it fell short of the mark—she swiped away the tears streaming down her cheeks. She would leave the letter in his bedroom away from the prying eyes of the staff. Then she would pack a few essential things for Heidi and Zoe and go to Polly's house until more formal arrangements could be made.

Slipping into a robe she padded into the hall, gazing around her.

She'd only been here for a few weeks, but already the castle was beginning to feel like a home. The warmth of the newly painted walls, the scattering of objects collected throughout her travels and the splashes of color and homey touches had helped her to bond with the huge house. Where once she had thought she would never feel comfortable, now she enjoyed its rambling halls and flowing layout.

She heard noises from across the hall and, peeking around the corner, she saw that Zoe and Becca were bent close together putting a puzzle together. The sight of the two little girls—identical except for their haircuts—tore at her heart. They'd had so little time together. The girls were just now beginning to bond with each other. If they'd been given more time…

No. She couldn't think about that now. As much as she might like to keep the girls together, she also knew that to keep them together for the sake of a dying relationship would only prolong the inevitable and increase the pain of a future parting.

She needed to make a clean break.

Today.

Farther down the hall, Cara slipped into Ross's bedroom, then stood still, absorbing the silence.

She missed him already. The scent of his cologne hung in the air along with the tang of his soap. Crossing to the closet, she stepped inside to finger the crisp white shirts, the elegantly tailored suits, and there at the far end, jeans, T-shirts and a stupid gorilla hat from their family trip to the zoo.

Without warning she began to sob—huge overwhelming sobs that welled up from the depths of her heart and tore at her fragile attempts to manipulate a situation which was already beyond her control.

In that instant she knew that she could never leave Ross Gifford. She loved him—more than she would have ever thought humanly possible. And whether or not he could ever care for her in return, she couldn't abandon him.

Not now.

Not ever.

Dropping to the floor, she wrapped her arms around her knees and wept as she had never wept before.

"CARA?"

Despite the fact that the Mom Squad van hadn't

been parked in the garage, Ross still called out to her.

It never ceased to amaze him how quickly his life had changed. Where mere months ago he had been rattling around in this house, completely miserable, now he was...

Happy.

He'd never thought he would ever be happy again. Granted, there were still moments when he felt a pang of loss. He had loved Nancy and he always would. But he also knew that she wouldn't have wanted him to grieve forever. She would have wanted him to feel joy.

Which was why, after a night of soul-searching, he had come to the conclusion that he was a fool. A complete and utter fool. He had happiness staring him in the face, and he was worrying about what might happen a year from now. Ten years. A lifetime.

A smile touched his lips, then a full-fledged grin. His partner probably would have told him that a night of lovemaking was responsible for his light-heartedness.

But Ross knew different. Granted, sex with Cara had been great. He'd never known a woman like her. She was so beautiful and elegant that she gave the impression of being reserved and a bit untouchable. Instead she was giving, spontaneous and full of surprises.

And she'd been more than patient with him while he'd been trying to get his act together.

What had he ever done to deserve her? Few men were given the opportunity to truly love and be loved *once* in a lifetime. But he had known the love of two good women.

Love. The word lodged in his head and Ross grinned again.

He never would have thought it possible. But yes, he was in love. He was in love!

The thought sent such a jolt of joy through his system that he couldn't contain it. Striding through the house, he took the stairs two at a time and rushed upstairs. As of this moment he was taking the rest of the day off. He would change into some comfortable clothes—maybe even put together the swing set that was still in its box in the garage. By the time Cara returned home from her errands, he'd have a good portion of it assembled.

''Cara, are you home?'' he called out as he reached the upper floors. He didn't really expect a reply since it was obvious that she and the children had gone somewhere, and Stibbs had left a note that he was shopping. It felt good to fill the silence with the sound of his own voice. Until Cara had filled his home with noise and laughter, he hadn't realized how silent and regimented his house had become. Even his children had been relegated to the far-off nursery. At the time, he'd thought he was offering them a safe, structured environment, but he saw now that he'd been wrong. The twins needed to regard the whole house as their domain, not just the nursery. They needed their pictures splashed over the refrigerator door, their crayons stashed in a drawer in his study and their tricycles rumbling through the hall.

And a swing set. They needed the biggest damn swing set he could build them. If need be, he could call his partner and enlist his help over the weekend. Maybe after the first unit had been put together, he and Peter could design a playhouse. Didn't little girls need a playhouse for tea parties and…whatever else little girls did?

Then there was Cara. What did Cara need?

He would arrange for the florist to send her some roses for one thing. And a ring. She needed a proper wedding ring. Would she like something traditional? Or something made to her own design? Maybe he could enlist Stibbs and Melba's help, maybe he could take Cara to Park City for the weekend. They could stay in one of the little bed and breakfast places, then hit the shops on historic Main Street. It would be a great way to show her how much he'd come to love her. And with the unconventional way their marriage had started, heaven only knew that they needed a proper honeymoon.

His exuberance filled him with an energy that he hadn't experienced in ages. Stripping out of his clothes, he didn't even bother to hang them up. Instead, he tossed everything but his suit in the general direction of the clothes hamper. Then he dragged on a pair of jeans and a T-shirt.

He was sitting on the bench fastening his tennis shoes when Ross saw a scrap of paper peeking up at him from beneath the row of charcoal-gray trousers. He was going to have to invest in some new clothes. He was tired of wearing nothing but gray suits and white shirts. Maybe Cara could help him pick out some snazzy ties, as well. He'd once had a reputation for his outrageous ties.

Bending, he snatched up the paper. Idly he opened it, wondering if he'd dropped the receipt for the swing set. But the moment the paper unfolded, the neat script leaped out at him.

Dear Ross,
There's no easy way of saying this. Heaven only knows that I've tried a dozen different ways to start this letter, but I've come to a point where I need to be honest—not just with you, but with myself as well. I was so sure

that we could make our relationship work, if
only for the children. But after last night I
know now that I can't go on. I think it's best
that we make a clean break. So today I'll pack
up my things and take the children with me
to Polly's. After that I'll contact my lawyer
about a divorce. I'm so sorry, but I discovered
I couldn't live loving you and not being loved
in return…

The strength drained from Ross's knees, and he
sank onto the bench.

She was leaving him.

Cara wanted a divorce.

His eyes dropped to the paper he crumpled in
his hand.

"I discovered I couldn't live loving you and not
being loved in return…"

But he did love her—more than he ever would
have thought possible.

Cara didn't know that.

A mix of emotions rushed through him—panic,
loss and a very real fear that if he didn't make
things right, he would lose Cara forever.

Jumping to his feet, Ross castigated himself for
being every kind of fool imaginable. By ignoring
his love for Cara, he had denied himself the

greatest happiness he could have ever known. Instead, he had filled his life with the pain of regret.

Ross was striding through the upper hallway, gaining speed with each step until he was running down the staircase.

How could he have wasted so much time? If only he had been honest with himself, he would have seen that it wasn't grief that had kept him from loving Cara. It was fear. He'd been so intent on protecting himself from losing his heart again that he had selfishly hoarded his growing affection. And in doing so, he had chased away the one woman who could make him whole again.

If only…if only…

Ross snatched his keys from the counter, knowing that he couldn't waste time thinking about what he should have done. What mattered most was that he knew he had been wrong in thinking that he would never love again. His feelings for Cara were lasting and deep. Now, it was up to him to prove to her that he no longer thought of their marriage as a quick solution to a problem. Nor was it a short-term option. He had to make her believe that he loved her—now and for all his days to come. And if she would take him back, he would spend the rest of his life proving that to her.

Ross was thinking so hard about going to Polly's house and speaking with Cara, that he nearly didn't notice the door opening and the woman of his thoughts stepping inside. The moment his brain absorbed the fact, he tossed his keys onto the counter again, grabbed the shopping bag from her arms and set it aside, then hauled her tightly into his embrace.

"You aren't leaving me, do you hear? I love you, Cara. I love you more than life itself."

He felt her stiffen in his arms and rushed to explain. "I found the crumpled-up letter in my bedroom—"

"No! I—"

Drawing back, Ross placed his fingers over her lips. "Please. Let me say this first—and then you can offer me all the recriminations you can think of, if you want. But before all that, I need to tell you how much I love you, how much joy you've brought into my life. I'm a stubborn fool and I don't deserve you. I know that. I've been falling in love with you a little more each day, and I didn't tell you. I selfishly hoarded the feelings, afraid that if I spoke about them too quickly, I would discover that I didn't have the capability to love that way again. I swear to you, if you'll stay, if you'll give us a chance, I'll spend the rest of my life proving to you that I do love you."

Her eyes filled with tears, and he feared that he

was already too late. She had given up on them and their marriage.

"Please," he whispered, his voice growing choked. "Give us a chance."

She covered his lips with her fingers, then rose on tiptoe and pressed her lips to his own. When she drew back, she whispered, "I love you more than you will ever know." She grimaced. "My brief thought of leaving was abandoned almost as soon as I finished that letter." She bit her lip. "I meant to leave it in your room, but I must have dropped it and—"

He didn't allow her to say any more. She'd already told him everything he needed to know.

She loved him.

She meant to stay with him as his wife.

Bending, Ross kissed her—sweetly, passionately, knowing that he had been close to losing his salvation, his chance at true happiness, his other half. Squeezing his eyes shut, he drew far enough away to murmur in her ear, "I don't want you to think that I'm using you to take Nancy's place. I—"

"I know. The past few weeks have been hard for you. You've had to grieve her loss. But I also know that you have enough love in your heart for both of us."

Ross wrapped his arms around her, holding her

close. "I've been twice blessed. First in having our twins reunited under one roof...but even more by your love." He grinned, rocking her in sheer joy. "I think we should get married again."

"What?"

"Let's get married. This time we need the works—a cake, a reception, a band. That way there will be no doubts that ours is a real marriage, not simply a matter of convenience."

She laughed. "I don't think we need the pomp and ceremony to make things real." She kissed him softly, sweetly, then whispered, "We'll have every morning of the rest of our lives to do that."

Epilogue

Cara smiled, standing on tiptoe so that she could peer out the window positioned over the kitchen sink.

The backyard was a riot of color with children in parkas, hats and mittens running up the snow-covered hillside pulling sleds and inner tubes, or giggling madly as one of the many adults offered to take them for a ride on a snowmobile.

Cara had to give the twins credit. They'd wanted an outdoor birthday party where they could invite everyone they knew. Cara had tried to talk them out of it, citing the cold, but the girls had insisted. As if sensing the importance of the day, the weather had cooperated. The sun shone from a cloudless sky, and the temperatures hovered in the balmy forties.

From somewhere in the other room, a door

slammed, and children squealed as kids ran in and out of the family room where they could help themselves to hot chocolate or roast hot dogs over the fire. Balloons had been tied to every available surface and Mom Squad employees distributed ice cream and cake to the guests. Returning her attention to the twins, who were opening presents at the dining room table, Cara smiled as Zoe, Heidi, Becca and Brianne took turns unwrapping their gifts and proudly related to their friends how theirs was a special family just like those in the fairy tales.

Cara blinked at the tears that gathered behind her eyes at the girls' innocent remarks. If she needed a sign that the children were as happy as she, Cara had just been given one.

Returning to the stove, she stirred the pot of hot cocoa simmering on the back burner. She'd been there only a moment when a pair of strong arms slid around her middle.

"What's the matter, sweetheart?"

She smiled. She would never tire of Ross's open affection—just as she would never tire of his touch.

"Not a thing," she murmured, leaning into his embrace.

"Happy?"

"Incredibly happy."

Ross held her even more tightly against him, and she felt his lips brushing her hair. When his hand dropped to tenderly stroke the soft swell of her abdomen, she smiled.

"Is it time to make our own announcement to the guests?"

Cara blushed in delight and embarrassment, but since the twins had asked them time and time again for a baby brother, she saw no way to avoid the inevitable.

Flipping off the heat on the stove, she was about to join the rest of the guests when Ross turned her in his arms.

Her breath caught in her throat when she caught a glitter of tears in his eyes.

"I love you, Cara," he whispered, his voice raw with emotion. "I never thought I could love like this again. I never thought that I could be so blissfully happy and complete."

Throwing her arms around his neck, Cara clung to Ross, tearfully agreeing. Her life, her home and her future happiness were wrapped up in the heartstrings of her husband and her children. Granted, they'd had a rocky beginning, but she had no regrets for the events that brought them together, only a sweet assurance that they were always meant to be together.

"I love you, Ross Gifford," she whispered.

He looked down at her, his eyes radiant and warm. And in that instant she knew that whatever life had in store for them, they would always have this. A love that would last forevermore.

There's a baby on the way!

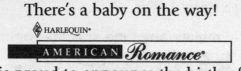

is proud to announce the birth of

AMERICAN *Baby*

Unexpected arrivals lead to the sweetest of surprises
in this brand-new promotion celebrating the love
only a baby can bring!

Don't miss any of these heartwarming tales:

SURPRISE, DOC! YOU'RE A DADDY! (HAR #889)
Jacqueline Diamond September 2001

BABY BY THE BOOK (HAR #893)
Kara Lennox October 2001

THE BABY IN THE BACKSEAT (HAR #897)
Mollie Molay November 2001

Available wherever Harlequin books are sold.

Visit us at www.eHarlequin.com   HARBABY

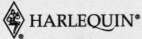

Harlequin truly does make any time special.... This year we are celebrating weddings in style!

A Walk Down the Aisle
WEDDING CELEBRATION

To help us celebrate, we want you to tell us how wearing the Harlequin wedding gown will make your wedding day special. As the grand prize, Harlequin will offer one lucky bride the chance to **"Walk Down the Aisle" in the Harlequin wedding gown!**

There's more...

For her honeymoon, she and her groom will spend five nights at the **Hyatt Regency Maui.** As part of this five-night honeymoon at the hotel renowned for its romantic attractions, the couple will enjoy a candlelit dinner for two in Swan Court, a sunset sail on the hotel's catamaran, and duet spa treatments.

Maui • Molokai • Lanai

To enter, please write, in, 250 words or less, how wearing the Harlequin wedding gown will make your wedding day special. The entry will be judged based on its emotionally compelling nature, its originality and creativity, and its sincerity. This contest is open to Canadian and U.S. residents only and to those who are 18 years of age and older. There is no purchase necessary to enter. Void where prohibited. See further contest rules attached. Please send your entry to:

Walk Down the Aisle Contest

In Canada
P.O. Box 637
Fort Erie, Ontario
L2A 5X3

In U.S.A.
P.O. Box 9076
3010 Walden Ave.
Buffalo, NY 14269-9076

You can also enter by visiting www.eHarlequin.com
Win the Harlequin wedding gown and the vacation of a lifetime!
The deadline for entries is October 1, 2001.

HARLEQUIN®
Makes any time special ®

PHWDACONT1

HARLEQUIN WALK DOWN THE AISLE TO MAUI CONTEST 1197
OFFICIAL RULES
NO PURCHASE NECESSARY TO ENTER

1. To enter, follow directions published in the offer to which you are responding. Contest begins April 2, 2001, and ends on October 1, 2001. Method of entry may vary. Mailed entries must be postmarked by October 1, 2001, and received by October 8, 2001.

2. Contest entry may be, at times, presented via the Internet, but will be restricted solely to residents of certain geographic areas that are disclosed on the Web site. To enter via the Internet, if permissible, access the Harlequin Web site (www.eHarlequin.com) and follow the directions displayed online. Online entries must be received by 11:59 p.m. E.S.T. on October 1, 2001.

   In lieu of submitting an entry online, enter by mail by hand-printing (or typing) on an 8½" x 11" plain piece of paper, your name, address (including zip code), Contest number/name and in 250 words or fewer, why winning a Harlequin wedding dress would make your wedding day special. Mail via first-class mail to: Harlequin Walk Down the Aisle Contest 1197, (in the U.S.) P.O. Box 9076, 3010 Walden Avenue, Buffalo, NY 14269-9076, (in Canada) P.O. Box 637, Fort Erie, Ontario L2A 5X3, Canada.

   Limit one entry per person, household address and e-mail address. Online and/or mailed entries received from persons residing in geographic areas in which Internet entry is not permissible will be disqualified.

3. Contests will be judged by a panel of members of the Harlequin editorial, marketing and public relations staff based on the following criteria:

   - Originality and Creativity—50%
   - Emotionally Compelling—25%
   - Sincerity—25%

   In the event of a tie, duplicate prizes will be awarded. Decisions of the judges are final.

4. All entries become the property of Torstar Corp. and will not be returned. No responsibility is assumed for lost, late, illegible, incomplete, inaccurate, nondelivered or misdirected mail or misdirected e-mail, for technical, hardware or software failures of any kind, lost or unavailable network connections, or failed, incomplete, garbled or delayed computer transmission or any human error which may occur in the receipt or processing of the entries in this Contest.

5. Contest open only to residents of the U.S. (except Puerto Rico) and Canada, who are 18 years of age or older, and is void wherever prohibited by law; all applicable laws and regulations apply. Any litigation within the Province of Quebec respecting the conduct or organization of a publicity contest may be submitted to the Régie des alcools, des courses et des jeux for a ruling. Any litigation respecting the awarding of a prize may be submitted to the Régie des alcools, des courses et des jeux only for the purpose of helping the parties reach a settlement. Employees and immediate family members of Torstar Corp. and D. L. Blair, Inc., their affiliates, subsidiaries and all other agencies, entities and persons connected with the use, marketing or conduct of this Contest are not eligible to enter. Taxes on prizes are the sole responsibility of winners. Acceptance of any prize offered constitutes permission to use winner's name, photograph or other likeness for the purposes of advertising, trade and promotion on behalf of Torstar Corp., its affiliates and subsidiaries without further compensation to the winner, unless prohibited by law.

6. Winners will be determined no later than November 15, 2001, and will be notified by mail. Winners will be required to sign and return an Affidavit of Eligibility form within 15 days after winner notification. Noncompliance within that time period may result in disqualification and an alternative winner may be selected. Winners of trip must execute a Release of Liability prior to ticketing and must possess required travel documents (e.g. passport, photo ID) where applicable. Trip must be completed by November 2002. No substitution of prize permitted by winner. Torstar Corp. and D. L. Blair, Inc., their parents, affiliates, and subsidiaries are not responsible for errors in printing or electronic presentation of Contest, entries and/or game pieces. In the event of printing or other errors which may result in unintended prize values or duplication of prizes, all affected game pieces or entries shall be null and void. If for any reason the Internet portion of the Contest is not capable of running as planned, including infection by computer virus, bugs, tampering, unauthorized intervention, fraud, technical failures, or any other causes beyond the control of Torstar Corp. which corrupt or affect the administration, secrecy, fairness, integrity or proper conduct of the Contest, Torstar Corp. reserves the right, at its sole discretion, to disqualify any individual who tampers with the entry process and to cancel, terminate, modify or suspend the Contest or the Internet portion thereof. In the event of a dispute regarding an online entry, the entry will be deemed submitted by the authorized holder of the e-mail account submitted at the time of entry. Authorized account holder is defined as the natural person who is assigned to an e-mail address by an Internet access provider, online service provider or other organization that is responsible for arranging e-mail address for the domain associated with the submitted e-mail address. **Purchase or acceptance of a product offer does not improve your chances of winning.**

7. Prizes: (1) Grand Prize—A Harlequin wedding dress (approximate retail value: $3,500) and a 5-night/6-day honeymoon trip to Maui, HI, including round-trip air transportation provided by Maui Visitors Bureau from Los Angeles International Airport (winner is responsible for transportation to and from Los Angeles International Airport) and a Harlequin Romance Package, including hotel accomodations (double occupancy) at the Hyatt Regency Maui Resort and Spa, dinner for (2) two at Swan Court, a sunset sail on Kiele V and a spa treatment for the winner (approximate retail value: $4,000); (5) Five runner-up prizes of a $1000 gift certificate to selected retail outlets to be determined by Sponsor (retail value $1000 ea.). Prizes consist of only those items listed as part of the prize. Limit one prize per person. All prizes are valued in U.S. currency.

8. For a list of winners (available after December 17, 2001) send a self-addressed, stamped envelope to: Harlequin Walk Down the Aisle Contest 1197 Winners, P.O. Box 4200 Blair, NE 68009-4200 or you may access the www.eHarlequin.com Web site through January 15, 2002.

Contest sponsored by Torstar Corp., P.O. Box 9042, Buffalo, NY 14269-9042, U.S.A.

PHWDACONT2

TRUEBLOOD, TEXAS

In September 2001 look for

HIS BROTHER'S FIANCÉE

by *USA Today*
bestselling author

Jasmine Cresswell

Lost

One groom. Emily Sutter is up to her
ears in the final plans for her lavish
society wedding when her fiancé
informs her that he can't marry her.

Found

A stand-in at the altar: her fiancé's black-sheep
brother. Emily assumes Jordan Chambers has saved
her from the embarassment of being publicly jilted
in order to salvage an important business merger
between their families. But Jordan's not motivated
by family at all. What he's always wanted is Emily,
and he's not about to squander his only chance.

Finders Keepers: bringing families together

HARLEQUIN®
Makes any time special ®